NO STONES UPTURNED

Subhashini Ramakrishnan

V&S PUBLISHERS

Published by:

V&S PUBLISHERS

F-2/16, Ansari road, Daryaganj, New Delhi-110002
☎ 23240026, 23240027 • *Fax:* 011-23240028
Email: info@vspublishers.com • *Website:* www.vspublishers.com

Regional Office : Hyderabad
5-1-707/1, Brij Bhawan (Beside Central Bank of India Lane)
Bank Street, Koti, Hyderabad - 500 095
☎ 040-24737290
E-mail: vspublishershyd@gmail.com

Branch Office : Mumbai
Jaywant Industrial Estate, 1st Floor–108, Tardeo Road
Opposite Sobo Central Mall, Mumbai – 400 034
☎ 022-23510736
E-mail: vspublishersmum@gmail.com

ISBN 978-93-815887-2-7
Edition: 2020

Printed at : Param Offsetters, Okhla, New Delhi–110020

Dedication

I dedicate this book to Natraj, Vijay and Vandana my pillars of support and strength and who have patiently taught me the reason to smile.

Acknowledgements

I extend my sincere gratitude to my Publisher and Editor of V&S Publishers for making my dream a possibility.

I thank my dear students who have been the real reason for writing this book, they are my true inspiration.

I thank my friends and well-wishers for constantly motivating me to follow my destination.

I thank the God Almighty for giving me the direction and courage to pursue and explore my ability as a writer.

Contents

Foreword

It was during my attempt at M.Phil when I realised that it was futile to write about another author and work on what others have said and written about them. It then struck that I must write my own book. The idea did seem interesting but when I had to compare myself with other writers, I felt inadequate and it took many years in-between, what with changing places, houses and schools, that I mustered the courage to take the pen and write the first lines.

I would often observe people while I waited at the railway station and admire the resilience that they possessed. I would look at a tired wife carrying bags and baggage while the husband sauntered ahead. I would notice the petulant youngster who would harass his mother for some eatable or something that he fancied and the sheer frustration on the mother's face. I couldn't help but notice the reluctant teenager who would follow his parent with a look of sheer boredom and helplessness.

With changing times, I would observe the people at the airport and marvel at almost the same scenes but with less companionship and graciousness, the passengers would show indifference to everyone around them and this would make it more interesting because the language would be English, the perfume, Chanel and the attitude, stiff upper class.

The market offered more such readings and there had been times when I would absentmindedly walk the market observing and noticing all that would happen around me and forget totally as to why I had ventured there in the first place!

The summer heat would take me to the malls and I would watch a lot more interesting sights and sounds. Noisy teenagers in fashionable and trendy clothes, the middle aged wearing modern outfit but with sterner faces and I would be exhilarated to notice the hustle and bustle around me. There was indeed a time when I had literally walked into a pillar since my eyes were glued on to an interesting person walking in front of me, very narrowly I had missed, hurting my head had my son not pulled me back in the nick of time!

I have observed life around me whether it was from a train or a bus or a plane, even in a car I would look out of the window while my driver drove (since I could not be trusted to drive, being absentminded about directions all the time) and I would enjoy the rides like a young child and thoroughly soak in the merry joy rides as I would call it. It has been these observations that have helped me to write this book.

My life has been one long travel so far, much of it I have lived in the north, a few years in the southern part of India and over the years, I have admired both the living atmosphere as variant, vibrant and absolutely charming to say the least. My experiences in these parts have taught me the differences in individual lifestyles, food habits and attitudes of the people of north and south. Although I admire the north for its dynamic approach to life and the absolute showmanship of the many people I have met, it's the sober and serene south that I love the most and maybe that is why the stories have a more than subtle touch of the southern flavour than its more vibrant counterpart up north.

We can do it if we believe we can and I believe in living in the moment. It's the pleasure that I get in small and short moments of life that has inspired me to pen down my thoughts and feelings. I also advocate the fact that stories need not necessarily be all about thrill, adventure or mystery; it could be about life, moments and living. At no point of time did I envisage that my written work belongs to any specific genre or category or age group. It is meant for everyone who can appreciate a tale told simply and shortly.

– Subhashini Ramakrishnan

Preface

The story ***Gold Chain*** is about a middle class family which prides itself for its ability to judge and justify every action of any individual with confidence and command. Sometimes people and times may not remain constant and we need to accept all that which happens in our lives with grit and hardiness.

Revelation follows the life of a staunch moralist who rigidly believes that his convictions are correct and the world would accept his dictum as final. Fate has it when he realises a forgone truth that it is he who needs to change and not the world for his sake.

Kaushy is a real life incident that happened to a young girl yet the fictional aspects added gives it a different flavour and setting. Medicine cannot help the mind if it chooses to wander and no one can really analyse, or comprehensively explain what the human brain can concoct.

When Times Change is the story of a woman as in a Diary entry. Although there are many such unsung heroes in our society today, no one really cares or shares the concerns of the common man/woman and they are left to fend for themselves.

God Bless My Darling is the story of a child who was unwell but with the support and sheer effort of her mother fights the battle to survive and sustain her life. It's the positivity that people show that makes life worth living.

The Night That Changed My Life is about a teenager who learns a thing or two about life in a short journey that she undertakes with friends and family. It is an eye-opener for the young girl who realises that the world is not what we assume or that it portrays.

The Green Grass is about a family which believes that their lives are worth emulating since they could realise their dreams, but when one's dream is fulfilled, it's time to create another dream and not to continue believing in the longevity of the dream to last forever.

Ambujam Mami is the story of a woman who, contrary to belief, is a strong and resilient person. We humans always typecast people into categories and sometimes it is carried too far, the world does possess many such people who break many a myth time and again and make us introspect about our ability to pass judgement.

Fit For A Queen treads into the life of a group of women who lead lives which is different and variant from each other, yet common enough to make them realise that while the wine remains the same, the bottle does differ from one to the other.

No Stones Upturned is about a teacher's journey. There is no moral message, just a chapter from the teacher's life, while he journeys from place to place and makes friends and well-wishers for life.

1

The Gold Chain

Krishnan held the chain lovingly in his hand. His father had handed to him one of his prized possessions. It was nearly fifteen years old and the Rudraksh was somewhat worn out. Krishnan rubbed the contours of the chain and tearfully recalled his father's words, 'take care of it'.

But fate however had other plans. Such reassurances are short lived, One day while removing his shirt, the chain inadvertently got entangled with his *'Janawera',* and when in all the humid hurry to take a bath, he had tugged slightly harder, he heard the ominous snap. Anuradha was in the kitchen, Krishnan ran to her and said:

"Oh! My God, it just broke." Anu rushed to console her crestfallen husband and said in a soothing voice:

"Shhhh... its okay, doesn't matter, we can get it repaired."

She quickly took charge and told him, "Coming Sunday, we will go to Parameshwaran and it will be just as good as new."

Laughing at her own pun, she took the chain and put it in the safety of the locker.

Meanwhile, Parameshwaran had arrived at his shop in Karol Bagh's *Vivek jewellers* that Sunday morning.

As he opened the door of his small shop, he thought how thirty-five years had passed.

He was twenty-two when he took the Chennai Express from Madras (Chennai). His family had travelled with him from Kalpathy in Palghat to see him off at the station. His uncle had promised him a job in Delhi at his jewellery store. His father's family had been *'Thathan'* for many generations. He could say that he was well-versed in the art of moulding the yellow metal. Having an eye for details had always been his vantage point. He would sometimes ask his sister to draw a *Rangoli* design and he would improve on it. He would then show it to his father who would scrutinise it; either grudgingly accept it with a grunt, nod or glare at him or simply leave it on his stool. He would then pick it up dejectedly and walk to the goldsmith and watch fascinated while they worked. He was told that new machines had started making the work easier and faster, but Parameshwaran knew that it would be a long time before he would be able to see any change in the small shop of his father in Kalpathy. After his second sister's marriage, money seemed to flow the way the *'Kalpathy puzha'* would flow in the summers.

The trickle was not enough for his other two sisters' marriage, let alone his education and the regular goodies at home that he had been accustomed to in all those years.

It was with great trepidation that his father had agreed to send him to Delhi to work at his brother's small shop in Karol Bagh and now it was thirty-five years since and Parameshwaran had become a true Delhiite. He had changed and adopted himself to the lifestyle of Delhi except his native Malayalam accent for which most of his north-Indian friends teased him and made fun of his *'madarasi'* twang always laughing and mimicking behind his back. He would sometimes get very angry, but would console himself by saying that after all, he was definitely not a native of these parts and therefore they were justified in doing so.

What's a casual banter between friends? Wasn't' he doing exactly the same thing behind their back at home during dinner mimicking their style, walk and talk and lifestyle? Yes! Life did have its ups and downs.

Parameshwaran, like many of his tribe, took all the teasing well in his stride but promised himself silently that his children would never have to face the slight, and true to his promise, his two sons took to Delhi and northern India like fish take to water.

They became engineers and by the grace of the good Lord had taken up jobs with corporate firms and had settled with their families in Mumbai and Hyderabad. Parameshwaran took pride in telling his friends that Anil, the eldest, had also been offered a posting at Norway and Ajay too was given the choice of India or the promised land of the United States of America.

When he opened the door to his shop that morning, he chuckled softly to himself that thankfully they had married good family girls from his community, unlike their other friends who had married into the local population leading a double life of managing North and South. Surely, he wouldn't have been able to adjust to the oily food and he was sure that they would not take kindly to coconut and coconut oil in all his food. His wife, Kamala had always stuck to the home cooking that he so much liked. In fact, his mouth started salivating when he thought of the hot *iddlys* and chutney with the wonderful aromatic *Sambar* that his wife had prepared for him in the morning. He made a mental note to call his wife and ask her about the lunch that she planned for the afternoon. While ruminating, he dusted his table and adjusted his spectacles, and remembered his father who had passed away to his heavenly abode the previous year.

Parameshwaran could never go back home and somehow realised his Parent's loneliness and pain. They had refused to stay with him in Delhi, because it was impossible for them to bear with the torturous winter and the scalding summer heat that Delhi is infamous for, they would much rather live in their small but comfortable house in Kalpathy than suffer the inclement weather in the capital city.

Parameshwaran and his wife would visit them instead every year and spend a month or so in their ancestral house. It was always refreshing to get away from the dusty streets of Delhi to the humid, yet clean air of Palakaad. His father's death left him richer by twenty three lakhs after selling the property, but it also sealed off his reason to return. His mother had decided to stay with her brother in Palakaad. He now belonged to Delhi and when his sons borrowed the money that he had for setting their own houses in Hyderabad and Mumbai, Parameshwaran was left with very little. After all, his children's needs were greater than his own, he argued with his wife whenever this topic came up. Maybe it was time for him to settle down with his son, Ani in Norway. He had never been overseas and Kamala would definitely benefit from the change.

Business wasn't booming, so to speak, and his only remaining goldsmith, Narasiman, had not been coming regularly.

When Parameshwaran had started the business taking the reins from his uncle who did not have any children, he was well-known in the South Indian circuit. He was usually given the job of getting the bridal jewellery ready in the traditional style. He also made small earrings for the one-year old kids on their birthdays and other such important occasions. Times had changed since then. Parameshwaran had been greatly pleased when he had acquired the shop from his uncle, but as his clientele dwindled and competition increased his spirit and his pockets had shrunk in size. People now wanted intricate designs and patterns and more variety. They wanted more for less and as the competitors were able to provide just that, he was definitely losing.

In fact, his shop had remained exactly the same but everything around his shop had changed. Gargantum structures overpowered his small shop and things just became out of proportion before his very eyes. If only he had appointed silk clad beautiful girls to work for him and maybe improved his shops aesthetics, then maybe, his business would have prospered like the rising gold price!

When Krishnan and Anuradha walked into his shop, he was contemplating along the lines of selling his shop, but when he saw them, he said to himself, 'maybe not yet'.

Krishnan showed his chain which Parameshwaran had made fifteen years back for his father and he proudly, held his artwork feeling elated.

"It will be ready in ten days," he declared beaming.

A content Krishnan walked out of the shop with the value of the gold written on a piece of paper, tucked safely in a small cover. The gold was safe and with its maker. Somehow, this made Krishnan feel comforted. Varun had sniggered in the morning when Krishnan told him that his father's chain was broken. Vani joined Varun and this lack of empathy in his children infuriated Krishnan, but now he was at ease. Anu wanted to buy some slippers from her favourite showroom and he had happily joined her in her quest for fitting footwear.

It was nearly two months since then and still the chain was not ready. Krishnan became slightly edgy when once again his phone call to Parameshwaran met with no response.

Meanwhile, Parameshwaran was waiting for Narasiman to come but his prolonged absence became a matter of concern for him. He approached his *Marwari* friend and asked him whether he could help; reluctantly, his friend agreed, promising no early date of delivery. A good two months later, the gold remained unattended.

Parameshwaran now used evasive tactics with Krishnan promising him further dates with emotional convictions.

Six months down the line, Krishnan panicked. He threatened Parameshwaran with legal actions. Gone were the good friendly camaraderie, only bitter and acerbic words were exchanged. Parameshwaran heard it all helplessly. When Narasiman appeared one day, Parameshwaran was relieved but when work really started, Narasiman again disappeared.

Three months later, excuses continued. Krishnan was far too hurt, why can't he trust his own people? Everything had changed so much. People playing games and finding excuses beyond belief. Krishnan had always taken pride in telling his colleagues in the office about how ethical south Indians are, saying no matter how they were, they never cheated.

He took pleasure in sharing his delectable *Rice Sevai* and other authentic dishes that Anu made for him to be shared in his office. He would snide at the 'go easy life' of his friends in the office and would say how a south Indian would never do anything against his principles. In his list of transgressions, cheating stood at the bottom of the ladder .

Now all those words seemed like empty and noisy wisdom which was meaningless. Parameshwaran had been playing hide and seek for a year now and he did not know what to do.

Should he call the police? How can he take the aid of the law against Parameshwaran, wasn't he an old acquaintance?

NO! Not done. A defiant Krishnan called his mother in Chennai to call up Parameshwaran using emotional pressure.

Thirteen months and eight days later, when a much wizened, yet adamant Krishnan called Parameshwaran for may be a thousandth time, he was told to come and collect his item.

Parameshwaran weighed the gold dust and waited for the inevitable. He had told Krishnan to collect his gold. He couldn't repair it. It was time for him to move out of the shop, city and country. His life seemed empty of all his dreams, aspirations and efforts.

Krishnan arrived with his wife expecting certain results, vary, wry and totally flabbergasted, entered the shop and was greeted by a smiling Parameshwaran. Without much ado, he handed him a packet, weighed it on the scale and said that the gold was approximately the same, although not the way it was given to him. So saying, he handed Krishnan 6one thousand rupees with folded hands and his lowered penitent eyes begged forgiveness.

Krishnan choked with empathic emotion, accepted all that was given to him and left the shop in haste, lest his tears were noticed.

He saw that Anu's eyes were wet too. He had been unnecessarily harsh, remorse hit him strongly. Hastening to the car, Anu tucked at his sleeve and whispered.

"Why don't you check the gold?" Since all the papers had been signed, Krishnan had not realised that he had indeed not checked the contents of the packet. He slowly unwrapped the thin paper and as he opened it, a golden dust rose in front of his eyes and before he could do anything, the swirling wind left him standing alone at the end of the road with just empty paper in his hands.

2

Revelation

Vaidyanathan was fifty five years old but felt not a day older than thirty five. He would get up early in the morning, as early as 4.30 and do his *pranayam* and meditation for an hour and then go about his work. Getting ready was a ritual for him. The steaming cup of hot filter coffee that his wife, Jaya brought for him began his day and as he contently smacked his lips savouring the flavour of the coffee, he would decide the *modus operandi* for the day. His bath was a grand ritual in itself. After the refreshing bath which he would religiously take from a bucket and mug, he would smear the sacred ash upon his forehead and arms and touch it up with a small dot of red *vermilion* on his forehead, the sign of a *'Parama Shiva bhakth'*. After the daily ablutions, he would sit on his comfortable easy chair and read the morning newspaper occasionally calling out to his wife sharing with her the tragic and comic items of the news.

The metro card that he had procured gave him access to travel to Connaught Place in some comfort. As he said bye to Jaya, he considered how he had been concerned about the public display of affection so shamelessly exhibited by the youth and he had shook his head in disagreement with the present day youth and their callous indifference to the elderly.

He had often shared his worry about it with Jaya but had been met with little response.

He had told Jaya that he was proud of his children who never had even bothered to bring any such talks in the house, while Jaya had often told him that he must change his thoughts and ideals and adapt to the present generation. Vaidye was not conforming to such pseudo thoughts.

What is wrong with the generation today? He worried and headed for the metro station, hurrying slightly and fearing he would miss the 7.20 shuttle. He had read in the papers that the moral police would be on a lookout for such public display of affection also called PDA, and at this Vaidye was again not happy.

Why short forms for every word, Can't today's generation utter words in its pristine beauty?

He shoved his way into the metro. As he sat down he remembered his teacher, Mrs. Matthews, who would insist on not using any short forms. She elaborated on the virtues of words and the emphasis of the pronunciation and diction with such candor that it was a mesmerising experience for young Vaidye, so much that he would listen and savour every word uttered by her.

His station was announced and he quickly moved towards the exit, and then his mind wandered to the job at hand.

Mr. Gupta would be furious if he reached late and some days it was impossible for him to say a word in the edgeways, since Mr. Gupta was known for his erratic mood swings. Well today was no better. Vaidye hurried towards the *Gupta book house,* where he worked as a data entry operator for the publishing house. He had been working there for nearly ten years and every year, he would promise himself that he would quit, but it was always postponed for another year.

Expenses were high and the paltry sum of fifteen thousand that Gupta gave him grudgingly barely helped in making two ends meet. What with the educational expense of his daughter, her school fees since she was going to a fancy private school which fleeced the working middle class of its hard earned salary and other day to day expenditure.

Vaidye had often suggested that she should study in the government school where he had studied since the fees were much less than what he was paying for her and it had a better educational quality. Jaya had pointed out that the government schools had neither name nor fame and were definitely not right for their daughter.

"We never got such an opportunity; let our children at least get the best".

She had pleaded and that is why Vaidye had conceded to that emotional glassy look in her big black eyes, which would often melt his heart and make him feel weak in the knees.

Mr. Gupta was calling out his name and he quickly rushed to his seat.

"Mr. Vaidyanathan Gupta," was saying, can't you type anything properly? Why should you change the sentence?

If the writer wants the sentence in that order, why the hell should you change it to your convenience?"

"Oh! I forgot Mr. Vaidyanathan can't tolerate improper English. Am I right, Mr. Perfect?"

"Sorry Sir, I felt the need to correct the sentence..."

"You see the sentence should have the proper tense agreement..." What? You have no rights to tamper with any agreement Mr. Vaidyanathan!" Gupta shouted.

The writer is always right. We get paid to do their work not rewrite it for them. How many times should I tell you that? Get out of my sight and come back only when you have corrected all the errors and put it all back as it was!"

Vaidye walked back to his desk with the manuscript and knew that he had to retype almost all of the fifty pages that he had corrected and typed. It would be a long day.

The journey back was not so comfortable because of all the shoving and jostling in the metro and a tired Vaidye reached his house, a small two-room apartment.

It was almost a Mumbai kind of accommodation yet comfortable for Delhi standards. It was difficult and cold during the winters and his wife had often complained about her back ache and how the cold was unbearable.

He had, many a time, contemplated about going back to Chennai where at least such weather fluctuations would not happen. Heaters in winter and AC's in summers are a must in Delhi and their servicing also cost so much. Vaidye found it a struggle to make ends meet. In spite of much advice, his son, Kannan had managed to receive his degree in political science and had with great reluctance gotten his diploma in journalism and therefore, was now employed with a local agency, which was paying him a frugal salary, good enough only for his personal expense and his travel which was a thirty two km drive one way every day. He could contribute nothing to the family.

Vaidye was thankful that at least he did not have to pay for his expenses and studies anymore. His own cousins and their children were either doctors or engineers and Vaidye took great pride in telling his family about their posts and positions. Often he had inadvertently missed the look of remorse on Kannan's face when he ranted about his relatives.

It took Jaya all her strength to console Kannan and appease Vaidye with, "what is wrong with our children? After all, Kannan is earning, isn't he?"

This would shut him up for some time. Today he was in a lousy mood and Jaya was quick to see that. Giving him the hot cup of coffee, she went about telling him the gossip of their colony.

Mrs. Bakshi was again allowing her dog to bark all afternoon, wonder where she disappears during the day, while Jaya went on, Vaidye felt a vague pain in his stomach. He rushed to the toilet and when he got up to flush, he noticed blood in the commode. Worried he chose not to discuss this problem with Jaya. He could wait and watch. It could be because of the beetroot *Subzi* that he had eaten, he analysed.

Morning saw it worsen and the uneasy pain persisted. The day was long and the work unbearable. Once again the scene was the same at the end of the day. During the night, Jaya complained about blood stains in the toilet and that is when Vaidye told her about his problem. Jaya panicked and told him that he needed to visit the hospital.

Mr. Gupta was not so happy in giving his permission but grudgingly accepted, since Vaidye was definitely one of the finest workers he had.

In fact, he was happy that unlike so many of his other workers, Vaidye had not been very ambitious, or else he would have lost his best.

When Vaidye explained to his physician, Dr. Pandey immediately diagnosed it as grade three internal Hemorrhoids and told him that he needed surgery and informed him that he required advanced, and effective surgery which was minimal access and therefore, he would very quickly recuperate. Within twenty four hours he would be as good as new.

Reassured Vaidye asked how much it would cost him and to his dismay he was told that including room rent, OT charges, etc it would be a good one and a half lakh rupees.

Vaidye clutched his heart and Jaya took it hard, but both were aware that they had already kept a tidy sum for medical insurance.

"What is money if we can't spend it for our medical needs?"

So saying both went home and decided to use the Diwali holidays for the surgery. The following Friday, Vaidye got himself admitted and remembered the night before when he had become emotional and had assembled his family and told them rather too emotionally about what and how he had planned their future and his finances. He asserted rather strongly that everything would be with Jaya and she would be the deciding factor for almost everything.

His family had listened to him gravely and had acknowledged his wishes and promised that they would take care of everything. But it was in the hospital that Vaidye felt strange. He saw the magnitude of the surgery. What seemed so trivial for the doctors was a life saver for Vaidye.

It was maybe a routine duty for the doctors, but for him once in a lifetime experience. He felt alone and abandoned. Jaya fussed over him yet he missed his brother and his children. If only they were all there he would have felt reassured.

After the angry argument with his brother about a trivial insurance issue, he had promised that he would never talk to him and true to his promise; he had not talked to them for the past two years.

The hospital room beckoned menacingly and he realised how small and insignificant his life was in comparison to the vastness of the universe, the world, the country, the city and the hospital. A low wail rose in the next room and he realised the ailing gentleman in the other room had passed away. The hospital went about its job of writing the death certificate and as a matter of fact, the dead body was discharged to the relatives for the last rites. Do we really mean anything to anyone? He wondered about all those smses on his mobile phone about his getting well, or his friend's show of concern! Did they really care about his health?

He wondered what would happen to Jaya if he died at the operation theatre the following day.

Well! She would continue just as everyone else. His children – would they miss him? Or will they curse him and forget him because he was so strict with them all the time. He recalled all the acerbic words that he had uttered about almost everything which he did not like.

He had his opinions about everyone. He had a dislike towards people who enjoyed themselves. Vaidye had been a teetotaler all his life and spoke disparagingly about all those friends who smoked and drank? He was aware that Kannan too smoked but never in his presence.

What had he gained in life? No good job, little or no money, never a happy day when he had laughed or played with his children or his friends. Even the gods that he prayed seemed to have abandoned him that day. His remorse shook him up and he started crying. Jaya assumed that it was tears of physical pain and he allowed her to think so. What is the definition of pain he wondered? Is physical pain the only barometer of measuring pain or is it the mental torture, the magnitude varied he thought.

What he suffered now was unspeakable and as the medicine took him to his slumber, he realised that he had never done anything he wanted.

The surgery was successful the following day and when Vaidye woke up from the anesthesia he saw a concerned Jaya, Padma and Kannan standing around him. A warm glow of affection he felt for them. They were his family and all that mattered in his insignificant life was just them.

Vaidye was discharged a day before Diwali and when he entered his home, he promised himself that every moment of his life mattered, and there would not be any more tomorrow and it would be only for today that he would live. Change is the only constant factor and that is what his family would see.

A happy Vaidye, who would be always cheerful and cherish every moment of his day and make everyone happy, when applied the sacred ash on his forehead on the Diwali day, he thanked God for the most spiritual revelation that had been bestowed upon him.

3

Kaushy

Kaushilya worked as a servant in a house at Marar Road in Trichur. The old lady lived alone in that huge house and Kaushy would go early in the morning after a cup of hot tea that her mother prepared. Her brother was a bus driver and before he went for his duty, he would drop her in his cycle at the old lady's house and go on his way to the bus depot.

Kaushy was only fourteen years old, still like every other Keralite, she was neat and would change her clothes and fold them neatly in her bag and wear the work clothes which she would leave at the old lady's house every day. The lady lived alone in the huge house because she did not want to shift with her son in Chennai. She loved her freedom and her huge house provided her with all that she needed. She had nearly a hundred trees or so and they were mango, jackfruit and coconut in plenty all the year around. Kaushy marvelled at the bounty around her and would help the lady sell them to the condiment store when the harvest was in plenty.

During the jackfruit season, the area would have a sweet smell of ripe jackfruit and together with the old lady, Kaushy would help prepare jackfruit jam and mango pickles.

She had learnt all that from the old lady who would grudgingly teach her like an angry school teacher, but Kaushy would never mind because the old lady would allow her to take some home too and this would make her father very happy. Often the pickle making season would take longer than the regular time to go home.

So during those days, Kaushy would get to the short route home, which she was afraid to admit was frightening some times.

Her morning duties began at the old lady's house by clearing the front gate area and would make a beautiful *'kolam'* with white rice flour and decorate it with some seasonal flowers. She would sometimes admire her own handiwork and it would be a competition to excel from her neighbour who made larger *'kolam's* which would often cover almost the entire street facing their house. She would then go inside the house and would sweep and swab the floors and then get to the kitchen to cook. She would decorate the *'Swami'* room first since the old lady was particular about starting her morning *puja* which was an elaborate ritual of chanting *'Lalitha sahasranam'* followed by *'Shiva Stuti'* and other such long chants which Kaushy did not understand much. She would listen to the lady as she would go about her chores. It would calm her immensely.

Kaushy was a curious child and sometimes would wander here and there around the big house and the old lady would grumble and rant to her all the time.

"Kaushy! Make a simple *Rasam* with some curry today," the old lady would scream aloud and Kaushy would get to it.

The kitchen did not have any gas stove and she had to work on a pump stove to get her cooking started. It would burn on kerosene which Kaushy would procure from the vendor once a week. Often the old lady would accuse her of using too much fuel and grumble about the escalating cost of commodities. She would make surprise and stealthy visits to the kitchen just to check whether Kaushy was pocketing some expensive condiment from the kitchen. Bournvita and Elaichi were kept in the old ladys' room and the days when they were needed Kaushy would ask the old lady and would be grudgingly given.

After clearing off the vessels and setting the kitchen in order, Kaushy would clean the orchard of dried leaves and then go back to feeding the old lady her single meal which she would insist eating at eleven thirty every day.

Some days if it would get delayed, the old lady would give her hell and there would be no end to the grumbling for days to come. At twelve, Kaushy would eat the food left over after the old lady's meal. She would eat quietly without making any noise because the old lady would then be taking her afternoon snooze and if woken any time during her nap, demons would break loose.

Even the postman was forbidden to deliver letters at that time. Since the old lady was notorious for her bad temper and generous heart, most people would respect her request and not disturb her at that time.

By four, Kaushy would change and leave for her house. This she would do after making a cup of coffee for the old lady and then start on her journey back home. Her house was not far off and it would take hardly fifteen minutes to cross the small patch of dense greenery to reach her house. The rainy season would make the foliage impossible to penetrate and Kaushy would often find it difficult to navigate. When she was young, Kaushy would travel through these forest patches with her friends and play in the pool and puddle, and often her long skirt would be smeared with dirt.

Her mother would be there waiting for her and would scold her for her carelessness and would tell her to take any other route than the dense patch. Kaushy had ignored her all these years and would do what she wanted.

One day just as she was finishing her work and was getting ready to go home, she heard a rustling noise from the attic where the old lady kept a lot of old unused and almost useless items. She was of course forbidden to go there since she would in her mischievous best break something.

Since the old lady was sleeping, she tiptoed to the wooden staircase and climbed soundlessly. There were to her delight a whole lot of things lying there, an old chest which contained traditional Bharatanatyam dance dresses and bronze vessels which seemed difficult to lift. Old broken chairs and an old broken bed, but what caught her eyes was a portrait which lay hidden behind the cot. She pulled it out and noticed that the frame was good mahogany wood and it contained the portrait of a young man. His eyes captured her attention and Kaushy did not realise how long she had stood watching it.

'Where are you, you silly girl?' The old lady bellowed from her room.

Kaushy rushed down quickly dropping the portrait on the floor. The old lady was livid with rage and calming her with a cup of coffee, Kaushy rushed home.

Her mother was waiting and together they finished the daily chores at home before cooking dinner for the night. She could not go to school because her father who had a small teashop could not afford to send her to a private school. She had tried going to the government school till grade five.

Although the free food was a tempting, the learning was drudgery. So she had opted to stay at home and her parents had easily agreed. What was the point of higher education for her now? She could read and write, couldn't she? Anyway, she would be married soon.

In their area, electricity was a major problem and often people would eat dinner with the light of the day and sleep early since the work for them would start very early in the morning.

The morning rush was musical to Kaushy who enjoyed her day no matter what happened. It was symphony for her, the lady of the house sweeping the floor with a broom made of coconut leaf, had a scratching sound, the paper boy on his cycle with the bell ringing before dropping the paper at every doorstep, the rustling leaves, the crows on their flight and the sound of the world stirring around her fascinated her the most. It was magical.

Often she would marvel at the coconut cutter who would climb so high with a thick rope tied around his waist and reach great heights.

She would stand under the coconut tree watching the cutter disappear till she would be told to move away lest the coconuts that he would throw might fall on her head! Her mother would shout at her during the day telling her to stop gaping and snooping around and to do something useful instead.

"The girl simply is too much! What will she do in her husband's house I wonder?"

Kaushy of course never heeded to anything her mother said. But the afternoons were quiet and Kaushy missed the hustle and bustle of the morning, nevertheless even Kaushy with all her adventurous spirit was forced to take the old route everyday which often frightened her.

Then she saw him. He was wearing a white *dhoti* and he was bare-chested except for the gold chain that he wore around his neck.

His eyes were red and angry and he was glaring at her. He was lean and gaunt. A scar ran across his face and his lips had a perpetual grimace fixed on it. He followed her home and when she entered the gate of her house he disappeared. Kaushy did not give much thought to it then.

He was there today, Kaushy told her mother, but who is he? Her mother asked worried.

The last thing she wanted was a stalker for their daughter. Kaushy did not respond. Kamala was worried.

Yes, Kaushy was coming of age to be married. She had an oval face with bright big eyes and was quite tall for her age. Her long hair which Kamala braided everyday applying coconut oil and combing it lovingly fell up to her knees and when she walked her anklet made her presence a pleasant announcement. Kamala sighed, money was sparing and no matter how hard they worked, it was difficult to make both ends meet. How can they consider Kaushy's marriage now? Her husband had spent all their savings on a useless business venture and now they were struggling to stay away from the moneylenders. Her own arthritis had rendered her useless to work in any house and they had to send Kaushy to work. The old lady was alone and she seemed harmless enough, so it was okay to send Kaushy to work in the house.

Now a man was following her. "Was he making any gestures?" Kamala asked.

"No, no, he did nothing of that sort, he simply followed me home. When I turned to see, he wasn't there," said Kaushy matter-of-factly.

"Well in that case I will ask Krishnan to accompany you this Sunday when he has his weekly off."

This settled it. The following Sunday when Krishnan accompanied Kaushy from the old lady's house, there was no one following her.

Matters came to a head when Kaushy screamed,

"He was glaring furiously at me," Kaushy ran out of breath as she entered the house.

When Kamala went to check, there was no one. Kaushy was becoming strangely agitated and every day, she was becoming more afraid to go to the old lady's house. Then one day, Kaushy came dazed and simply fainted when she entered the house.

Kamala took her to the hospital and when she was being checked, all kinds of thoughts crossed Kamala's mind.

Is Kaushy safe? Oh God! Has she been raped?

And fear gripped her as she waited for the doctor's verdict. Her fears were unfounded. Nothing was wrong with Kaushy. With some medicines for weakness, the doctor dismissed her case.

The following week things did not improve. Kaushy became weak and afraid. She would jump at any sound and had the look of a captured dog around her. The local *Tantric* took a good look at Kaushy and declared that she was possessed. He flung sacred ash at her face and blew furiously. Kaushy coughed but remained the same.

He was about to pick a short stick and looked menacingly at her and was about to hit her stating that it was the only way to drive away the spirit, Kamala decided to intervene. She told the *Tantric* that she would find some other means. Kamala's brother suggested that she should take Kaushy to the Shiva temple at *Vetriviza* near *Ernakulum* and Kamala made plans for the weekend to do so. Strange stories of girls being possessed by demons were making rounds and Kamala had herself seen with her own eyes, the neighbour's daughter being treated by the village priest.

It was terrible and the sound that came from that house was awful. Kamala never wanted anything like that to happen to her daughter.

Kaushy slept all the way in the bus and when they reached the temple, she became agitated and highly excited. The Shiva temple was situated 30 km away from Ernakulam. It was believed that people who were mad or people who had been under the control of evil effects set on them by black magicians would get cured at that temple. Such people were brought to the temple during the previous night itself.

Then after the evening *puja* of the temple, they would attend the saffron *(kuruthi)* worship to the *Bhootha kala Yakshi* which was outside the temple.

Legend has it that there was a very dense forest in that area belonging to the *Arakkal panikkars*. There was a pond in the forest which had lots of tortoises. A group of hunters called *Ulladaas* used to catch these tortoises for their living. They would introduce a long sharp staff in to the pond and keep on hitting. Then the injured tortoises would come up. Then they would catch them. Once when a lady of their tribe was doing it, suddenly, she saw blood ebbing out of the pond. The entire pond became the colour of the blood. Then they started pumping out the water of the pond. After three full days of removing the water, they saw a stone in the bottom of the pond from which the blood was oozing out.

On the fourth day, a great sage came and applied some sacred ash on the wound. The blood immediately stopped. He told the people there to build a temple over the pond without removing the stone from that place. They filled up the pond, partially by sand. Even today, we can see the *Linga* only at the bottom of the pond, where water would be constantly oozing out. In rainy season, the idol would be covered by water and would not be visible.

Immediately after the temple was built, a mad man, belonging to the *Thalakkatt* family used to daily visit the temple. The devotees were afraid of him and prayed to the Lord to cure him. That day, one of mad man's family members was instructed in his dream:

"Tie up the mad man overnight. Next day, a new plant will appear near the temple. Collect one handful of leaves from this plant and hand it over to the priest. He would take out the juice inside the temple, mix it with cow's milk and do the *Pandeeradi puja* to the God, Then keep three *chakras* (The coin of Travancore) before the temple and take out the milk and make the mad man drink it. (The mixture would first become blue, then become dark red and then black, and later become yellow and then white.)

One hour after he drinks the milk, give him tepid water to drink. Then that mad man would vomit a lot. Then in the noon make him eat the *milk kheer (paal Payasam)* offered to the Yakshi. He would become all right." The temple has been following these rules from then on strictly.

Kamala and Kaushy entered the temple at forenoon and in the evening, the temple priest dressed in red *dhoti,* with a huge red *tilak* adorning his forehead came to her and told her to take Kaushy to the temple.

A strange ritual was taking place. The priest did an elaborate *puja*. He drew the ancient *Swastika* and then made inroads and poured water into it. The red colour of the vermilion mixed with the common dust of the ground made it look like blood and Kaushy was mesmerised by the same. He did all this as he was chanting a strange *mantra* which was drowned by the drum beats and the effect it had on the devotees was equally strange. Was it the drum beat or was it the *mantras*, Kamala wondered?

A young woman who was standing quietly suddenly started dancing on her own rhythm and Kaushy watched her hypnotised. The man standing next to her started crying and did not stop for a long time. The priest went on with his ritual heedless to the noise around him.

When the *puja* got over Kaushy looked pleased. The priest instructed them not to eat anything during the night and told them that they needed to keep their stomach empty for the morning rituals.

While going around the temple as a *parikarama*, Kaushy noticed a huge bull and stood their looking at it for some time. Kamala was tired and soon dozed off in the small enclosure that had been allocated to them for sleeping within the temple complex.

Somewhere during the night, when she woke up to go to the toilet, she noticed that Kaushy was missing from her place of rest. Panic-stricken she ran around the dark temple and when she came to the bull's enclosure, she saw Kaushy sitting there and looking at it strangely. Had it not been for kaushy's anklet, Kamala would never have been able to make out her presence. The strange almost glazed look in her eyes made Kamala weak in the knees and chanting *Shiva Shiva,* Kamala dragged Kaushy to bed.

Kaushy told her that the bull reminded her of Lord Yama and he seemed to be riding on the bull. He was calling her to join him. Deeply disturbed, Kamala slept the rest of the night sparingly.

The morning saw an elaborate ritual at the entrance of the sanctum sanctorum. Kaushy and the other devotees who had come for this ritual were made to drink a colourless liquid and were told to take *parikaramas* around the temple drinking warm water on the way as many times as they required. After about five rounds and seven glasses of warm water, later the retching started. Everywhere the devotees started vomiting and it became unbearable to watch. The relatives who had accompanied the ailing persons were in a state of shock themselves, but stood by them and after nearly two hours of having taken the medicine, calm descended around the temple.

Taking a bath again and changing into spotless white sari, the devotees then visited the temple and with the sacred ash and vermilion from the temple, Kamala returned home with Kaushy.

A black thread was to be worn around her waist all the time and was told to chant certain *mantras* during the day and night.

At home, her husband had finally realised that he needed to be the man of the house and had fixed Kaushy's marriage to his friend's son, who was also a bus driver. Kaushy did not react much to this information and listlessly went about her daily chores as usual. There was a drastic change in her and Kamala regretted ever scolding the girl for her vivaciousness now that all light and enthusiasm had gone away from her.

Kaushy went with her brother to the old lady's house to collect her salary and there lying outside the gate was the portrait. The old lady was clearing the attic since strange noises were coming. Assuming that there were some rodents on the prowl, she had got it cleaned. The picture made Kaushy stop short in her tracks and when Krishnan asked the old lady about it, she told him that he used to live in the same house before she had bought it and died of strange circumstance, since his body was never recovered. Kaushy did not speak much.

Fifteen days before her marriage, Kamala told Kaushy to go to the old lady's house and this time invite her for the marriage. Maybe, she would give some money which would definitely help for the marriage. The old lady was at her acerbic best and grumbled about all the work that she had to do alone and asked whether Kaushy would return to work again.

Kaushy said she would think about it and when the lady gave her a hundred rupees, she just took it without saying much.

Kaushy took the same turn which she usually did and just as she heard the crack of a twig under her feet, she turned and then she saw him. He followed her now and Kaushy ran as fast as she could. It had rained rather heavily the previous day and everywhere it was slushy and muddy. When she reached the dense foliage, Kaushy held on to the tree for support, while she caught her breath. She slipped all of a sudden and the soft sand pulled her down. She groped for some grip but couldn't. As she struggled to gain her composure, she saw the hand rise from the mud and clutch her feet. Kaushy fainted.

When she regained consciousness, she was in her house. She overheard the conversation that was taking place in the other room. They had found Kaushy lying there in the mud and right under her feet were the remains of a man. It was identified by the ring as the young man who had died of mysterious circumstances. It seemed that the young man had been murdered by his friends (who had committed the crime) and had buried him at the secluded place, and then had disappeared into the city. So when the old lady bought the house, nobody suspected what could have happened since the friends had spread the rumour that the young man had run away with a woman of another caste and would not come back. The wronged man was given a proper burial and soon Kaushy regained her old self again.

Kamala joked about the entire incident saying that her daughter had jumped from childhood to womanhood directly. Maybe she had been chosen by God to show the right path for a lost soul.

Much has changed since then and now Kaushy is happily married. She lives with her husband near the old lady's house. She is presently working at a sari store as a sales girl. Even today, when she takes the old route, she turns her head back just once to check whether she is being followed.

4

When Times Change

Dear diary

I was twenty four when I married into the well-to-do Chopra family at Agra. I came expecting like all brides, a very romantic, happy life. Movies had woven their magic in my heart and mind, and I felt like the bride who dreams of a fairy tale life. Today when I think back, how naive, unconventional, gullible and vulnerable to the core I was.

Like almost all girls of my age, I too had studied at a government school ensuring just about the basic education, where things like future work prospects or job opportunities did not matter. A good family name, a reasonably caring husband, house, gold jewellery and diamonds of course, were the dreams of any girl. I was no exception. My father owned a cloth store in *Jalandar* and I could say with pride that he was a well-known businessman in his circle, and people looked up to him in our Punjabi community.

I was fair and good looking, a prerequisite for any Punjabi girl. A fair girl could get for herself a good looking and a well to do Punjabi boy easily. Some of my friends, who were rather wheatish in colour were unable to rope in a good match, primarily because they were not fair.

Well, I did feel sorry for them but deep down I also felt happy that at least I did not have any such issues.

My marriage to Dharam Chopra was a dream come true. He was good looking and fair and tall, he was all that I had ever dreamt of. I pinched myself when I saw him for the first time and my happiness knew no bounds when the match was finalised. I recalled those wonderful days when I pranced the house feeling romantic and mushy.

Those were the days. One can only recall the innocence of those times. Well I often wonderd much later in my life why no one wrote about the 'happily ever after days' and what really happens is never shown, spoken or shared. The Chopras like my father had been residents of Lahore before partition and during the turmoil of the partition, had shifted to Delhi. They had been given a refugee status and were made to stay at Red Fort where the make shift contraptions were created for them. Slowly many of them had moved to different cities looking for employment and the Chopras too had built their empire at Agra. They were renowned businessmen of Agra. After the initial euphoria of marriage and the bliss of family life and learning, reality hit me rather hard.

Dharam was a good husband but like all businessmen, he would come late to the house at night. He was of course concerned about the household problems, my dalliance with my mother-in-law and my brother-in-law. I gloated about every issue and overemphasised with gusto and poured my heart out, he would listen to patiently and sometimes would fall asleep as I raved and ranted into the night. It worried me that he could not spend much time with me. I understood perfectly well that he had responsibilities, what with he being the eldest in the family and all that, but the fact that he had taken to drinking in a big way and remained drunk often worried me more.

When Prem got married I thought that I had company to gossip and complain about our mother-in-law but it turned out that Neha came from a rich and educated family of businessmen and she was more interested in working and to top it all, she spoke fluent English and almost always shunned my company. I had overheard her talking on the phone to her sister in Canada as to how she was unable to tolerate my rustic nature and behaviour. I was hurt and relegated myself to being useful in the kitchen which remained my domain for many years to come.

Well that was the time when I realised that I was truly alone in the house. I had been told by my mother on the day of my marriage that I should never call them to complain and any calls that they receive should be about some good news, festivals, etc, and true to that promise, I had hardly called them up. Even when I had visited them in the following years I had never shared my loneliness, my pain, or solitude and the indifference shown towards me by my husband's family. I had become quiet and withdrawn into myself.

Nikhil and Nikitha, my darlings, when they were born brought some happiness to my life. A turning point came when Prem and Neha decided to take their twins and live in an apartment which was closer to Neha's parents house. The house being small was given as the major reason for the shift. Life continued with the same pace, but then I had my children to keep me engaged and occupied. When Nikhil and Nikitha were studying in grade nine and ten that was the time when my mother-in-law passed away.

I was sad and unhappy, but also relieved that I did not have to take care of the invalid who would abuse me and scold me when she had bed-sores from lying in the bed for a long time. I, of course kept all my feelings to myself since I never had a sympathetic ear to share.

My father-in-law became more aggressive and angry at his loneliness and his angina attack had kept him away from drinks and non-vegetarian food that he so loved. He would remain grumpy and angry all the time and since I was available in the house always, he would make me the target and I would be at the receiving end of his abusive torrent.

Life would have continued in its own salubrious way had Prem not come one day to our house claiming that he wanted to shift back with them because the rented house was becoming cluttered since he had another son apart from the twin boys. He assured us that they would construct the upper floor and they would in no way interfere with our life. It went without saying that *Papaji* would remain with me since I knew his medicine timings etc.

Six months of headaches, backaches and mental torture later, the portion was ready and the Prem's moved into it. I could only recollect the painful times since Neha was also working and taking care of the business. After all, she was educated and equipped to fight the battles of life better than I could ever imagine. So I would often be left to take care of the children and like myself, Nikhil and Nikitha always ended up at the losing end. Neha's twins were used to hostel life and were able to fight and survive with cunningness and got away with almost anything they did.

Nikhil would come to me crying and complain about what the twins did, but I would calm him saying, "its ok they are brothers and fighting was not to be complained about." I recalled the fateful day when Dharam came home crestfallen stating that the shop was now facing stiff competition and business was really crashing.

Prem had been a saviour that day when he had proposed a construction company to be shared and managed together so that they can happily work and live together. I had shed warm tears of gratitude that day and it all seemed well when the business took off and Prem took the reins in his hand. Dharam was new to this area and had to often turn to his brother for advice. Neha had always been civil and distant, and once again my loneliness became acute. Nikitha had noticed my agony and had now taken upon herself to console me in my moments of frustration.

When Nikitha left for her graduation studies to Pune, I felt the loneliness biting into me. Dharam was becoming increasingly angry and frustrated. Small skirmishes were happening in the office, where Prem was deciding almost everything without consulting Dharam about it. He would drown himself in his Patiala peg toying with his large drink, sulking and brooding over his situation. No amount of cajoling from me brought him out of his drunken stupor.

Nikhil was grasping the situation, but refused to comment about it and somehow maintained a safe distance from his uncle and his boys. The day my father-in-law passed away, the family finally disintegrated. The unspoken words spoke louder than the silence around them. Nikitha timed it well enough to announce that she wanted to get married and the boy was a Sindhi with whom she had been studying in college and yes, she was decidedly marrying him and no one else. The marriage was solemnised at Jaipur and turned out to be a short family affair. The customary Punjabi dance was all there but something like the spirit was lacking.

Three months later, when Nikitha and Aman came to take their blessing, I broke down. I was losing one of my friends and with trepidation, I blessed them. Nikitha's departure to Dubai also saw in its wake more rifts in the business. The tension in the house was increasing and exhausting me. Nikhil was becoming more belligerent. I was perpetually worried and my hair had greyed beyond recognition. I had put on much weight and so had promised myself that I would stop eating non-vegetarian food after Nikitha's marriage. However now that promise seemed to have had a negative effect on me.

The once beautiful eyes had become dull and lifeless and my face had many more wrinkles than I remembered. A heavy paunch I had developed and somehow no matter how I tried, I was unable to change my sedentary life.

Prem came to our room one evening and broke the news. He told Dharam in no uncertain terms, that the business was suffering and both knew that Dharam was the reason for it. He brought out a proposal that Dharam could not refuse. He promised half of the property in terms of flats and other piece of land they owned and told him to take some share of the business and quit gracefully. The house he said he would like to keep since his family was definitely larger and at this, Nikhil got up to retaliate. I stopped him short and allowed Prem to complete his proposal.

A month later Nikhil was asked to join Nikitha in Dubai, where he could join the MBA course that he wanted to pursue and also help her in her small business which she had taken up with Aman's help. When Nikhil left three weeks later, I shut myself in my room for two days. A piece of my heart had somehow closed down forever.

A year later Nikitha happily announced her pregnancy and when I think about it I am sure I was the happiest at that time when I held the tiny hand of my grandson in my hand.

I felt reassured and content. Perhaps, life had much hope still.

We were now living in a small flat when Prem called us one day and announced that his first of the twins was to be married in three months time and they needed us to help in the marriage. When I walked into my old house, I felt I belonged there and I flung headlong into the marriage preparation. Such contentment I can't explain, I also felt important and needed. Returning after the engagement party, Dharam was in a happy mood and we played music and danced till two in the morning. When we finally hit the bed it was rather late and I went into a deep slumber. It was the silence that woke me up and I suddenly sat bolt upright. Dharam was not next to me and as I called out his name I checked whether he was in the toilet and when I saw no light I tiptoed to the other room and there in front of the fridge, Dharam lay lifeless. The hospital declared him brought dead and the following days remain a haze to me.

When Prem suggested that he would much rather postpone the marriage than have it in this mournful atmosphere, I disagreed and said that it was Dharama's dream to see his nephew get married and it must be conducted as planned. Nikhil and Nikitha made a feeble attempt to show their happiness but were not successful.

Aman called and told me to pack my bags and come and live with them at Dubai. What was there for me at Agra anymore?

It was decided that I would board the flight the day after the wedding. Almost all of Agra was there for the wedding and it was a grand affair. I cried silently missing Dharama's presence and hid my tears, lest it should spoil the celebrations. Whenever emotions choked me, I would excuse myself from the ceremony.

The day after the marriage, while the house was reverberating with the sounds of laughter and frolic, I bade farewell to my home of thirty years and as I climbed the steps of the flight, I was supposed to take, I saw my entire life pass by in that one fleeting moment and realised that my life held no great significance and everything I owned and belonged to now had severed itself from me once and for all. In another place, time and country, I had to get my footings and maybe my life there might have more meaning than what I was leaving behind. Times have changed indeed!

I am Sarita Chopra and I am signing off. Bye!

5

God Bless My Darling

Satya woke up to a throbbing pain in her body. Fever persisted during the day and continued with vomiting. When the doctor diagnosed viral infection and also recommended blood test, the waiting for the results and the pain just became too intense to bear. Nalini felt that something was wrong with her thirteen year old and prayed that nothing should be amiss. There are times in our lives that we pray to God hoping that things should not go wrong, deeply realising that no matter how much one prayed even God would not be able to salvage the situation, if we are so destined.

Nalini's heart sank when she was told that Satya had Meningitis and needed to be shifted to the hospital. She had no idea how this could have happened to her baby. Lately Satya had lost appetite and was averse to strong light in the room. The doctor confirmed the worst nightmare to follow. Nalini had always believed that faith and hope are the strongest human ability to sustain any adversity and she believed that she could help her child no matter what, and had hope in medicine and faith in her prayer to do so.

The following weeks in the hospital were intense yet Nalini had promised that she would not cry. How could she take care of her young son and old mother-in-law if she broke down?

Her husband did all that was possible to keep the money flowing and checking the arrival of relatives in and out of the hospital. Two weeks later, when she was told that she could shift Satya home, Nalini was relieved as she could take care of her baby her way. That night Satya slept peacefully and the following day showed interest in food.

The doctors had warned her that it might recur and in many cases, it could be life threatening but Nalini believed that she could help her daughter and definitely fight death if she really had to. After all Lord Yama couldnot be cruel to her!

When the night came this time, Satya was wide awake and smiled weakly at her mother.

"Amma can you tell me a story?" Satya asked.

Of course my dear, but take your medicines first and then I would read you some stories.

She began by reading short passages from PG Wodehouse and moved on to Agatha Christie. It was the story, 'Ordeal by Innocence' that saw the sparks of curiosity in Satya and Nalini was challenged to continue reading and questioning.

"Who do you think committed the murder?" and pat came the reply, "judging by the author's writing style it wouldn't be the one in prison, definitely someone at home".

Nalini was surprised by the agility of her brain and unravelled to her the complicated plot.

"Mom why not some new story today?" asked Satya and then Nalini realised that she had actually been reading about gem stones and had suddenly come across an idea to write a story which she was planning to read it to Satya for her opinion, but couldn't do so since everything became topsy-turvy after Satya's sudden illness.

So the following night, she handed Satya her written manuscript and Satya decided to read it this time for Nalini to listen.

THE BULLION TRIAL

The Quest

Goldie woke up with a start. She had the same nightmare, the black hooded man was following her and she was running into the darkness. It always began with the black eyes following her and then the chase. She shook herself awake. This got to end someday. Maybe she should pray, but not today, not now.

"I will leave today," she thought to herself.

As the day progressed slowly, it was a blur to her and by evening, she had taken a few things and was all set to go. The carefully laid plans went without a hitch and when she was safely out of the boundary wall without arousing any suspicion, she looked back once towards the formidable fort Knox of fortune, sighed deeply and moved away. It was home that she was leaving behind.

When she turned, she was face to face with an old man. He must have suddenly come up there for she had not seen him. His white hair and a glowing face attracted her instantly to him. She smiled and so did he.

"Where to, my young lass?" he asked somewhat breathlessly. Father *Pedro* beamed at her.

"I don't know father, anywhere but far far away from here," Goldie answered looking lost.

The wise father nodded his head as if he somehow knew the answer.

"Remember child, the road ahead is dangerous and do remain calm whenever you make any decision. I live in the church over there, come to me whenever you want" saying so Father *Pedro* turned to leave.

Goldie moved on. The world outside beckoned breathtakingly.

The journey

The honking of the car horn brought her back from her reverie.

She saw a smart young man in a translucent shimmering yellow shirt, even his eyes were of the same colour! Weird Goldie thought.

"Toby is my name, and for your service I came." He touched his cap ever so lightly and opened the door of the big limousine.

While she wondered just how he knew her and who had sent him, he said,

"Shall we go Madame?"

"Yes let's go," she answered promptly. He drove her through the streets where huge buildings with big hoardings winked at her seductively.

"You can invest in shares and stocks if you like. May be the hotel industry would interest you?" Goldie wondered what he was talking about.

Well! He doesn't matter. She could see everything and he did seem like a nice guy. While he chatted amicably, Goldie thought of Damien. She should have told him. She missed his firm and sensible advice but she wanted more, so here she was on her quest, her Journey into the unknown. It was exciting and thrilling, but he did mean the world to her.

"The industries seemed to have slumped due to the recent recession, I would suggest entrepreneurship," Toby continued while Goldie listened and just as suddenly, he stopped the car outside a huge building which had a sign which said, 'The gem star'. Toby took her to the office and as she entered, she noticed that everything in the office had shades of green and while she basked in the greenery, a tall gaunt looking gentleman walked towards her and guess what! He had worn a green suit and had beautiful green eyes.

He smiled genially and introduced himself as *EM Raldon* the owner of the gem star and yes! He would do business with her if she so wished. What did he sell, she had no idea!

Goldie excused herself with a promise to *EM Raldon* that she would get in touch with him as soon as possible. When she reached the car, Goldie realised that she had not eaten and was feeling hungry. Toby took her to a restaurant. Goldie instantly noticed the colour blue everywhere. Mr. *AG Marine* the manager came to her "Welcome Mademoiselle," his electric blue eyes captivated her.

A radiant smile stopped her in her steps as he accompanied her and as she waltzed through the three-course meal she felt warm and comfortable. Who said the way to a man's heart is through his stomach? A woman's heart craves for nothing less!

The small insignificant shop caught her fancy, while she travelled the length of the city and she entered the shop without further prompting.

The saintly looking *M Lazuli* smiled at her and as she gazed at the assortment of odd curios in his shop. A calm and serene feeling descended over her. *M Lazuli* spoke about spirituality and she felt herself transcending the realms of reality. The unscheduled stop over made Toby honk the horn unceremoniously and she quickly took leave promising *M Lazuli* about a long term association with him in the future.

While Goldie journeyed across the length of the city, a luminous light caught her attention and she walked into a dimly lit bar and even from a distance, she could discern his shock of red hair and as he came near, Goldie felt weak in her knees.

"Hi, wanna dance?" his deep throaty baritone made her gape in bewilderment.

He swept her off her feet and as he guided her expertly into the dance floor, he looked into her eyes and said, "Marry me." Goldie was stunned and quickly took her hand away. As she backed from Rudy, she stepped over someone's toes and as she wheeled around to apologise, the black, immensely large eyes of *Bach Pierre* held her hypnotised.

"Good evening Madame," he spoke in a soft lilting voice.

Rudy pushed her gently and said furiously to the hooded hoodlum, "Pardon me sir but she is with me!" What followed was something Goldie never could forget.

A flash and a yell and Rudy fell on the floor. *Pierre* pulled her hard and she spiralled behind him like a bleating sheep to its slaughter. It was the same nightmare, only this time it was real. She tried to break from his clutches, but in vain. The more she tried the tighter he held on to her.

The alley seemed endless but just as she was about to give up the struggle, she saw a shining light at the end of the road. Damien stood in all his splendour, her knight in shining armour, resplendent with a brandished sword.

What transpired was a short battle. Bach Pierre lay at her feet begging for life, while *Damien* pulled her towards him, Toby held the car open and both clambered into the car and as the car raced down the streets, Goldie fell into a dreamless slumber. She knew now that Damien had sent Toby.

The circle of life

The chimes of the church could be heard over the city as *father Pedro* pronounced them, man and wife.

In the array of guests, Goldie noticed *Rudy* (his arm in a sling), Toby with his yellow cap and matching dress, *Mlazuli* and *EM Raldow* and Mr *AG Marine* smiling and beaming at her and many more, she had not been acquainted with, maybe another time and another adventure, she thought. While she looked up at the formidable dome of Knox she knew she was home.

The music played on as she laid her head on Damien's ample shoulder and sighed smugly. After all, Damien was a girl's best friend!

GLOSSARY

Goldie: The most sort after yellow metal ***gold*** which every man or woman dream to own

The ***United States Bullion Depository***, commonly called ***Fort Knox***, is a fortified vault building which is used to store a large portion of the US official gold reserve.

M Lazuli: ***Lapis Lazuli*** – Traditionally believed to increase mental clarity, virility and calm. It is believed to be useful in relieving depression and promoting spirituality

E M Raldon: ***Emeralds*** – Strengthens the owner's memory, quicken the intelligence and assist in predicting the future

Rudy: ***Ruby*** is said to give name, fame, virtue, vigour, warmth and commanding power to its user

Toby: ***Topaz*** – This is a stone of strength

A G Marine: ***Aquamarine blue*** – A symbol of beauty, honesty and loyalty

Father Pedro: ***Pearl*** – This symbolises love, success and happiness

Bach Pierre: ***Black pearls*** are desired by women due to the mysterious aura surrounding them

Damien: The wearer of **Diamond** is protected from the bad influences of evil

The Bullion Trial

–By Nalini Jayaram

When Satya finished reading, she dropped the paper and started clapping her hands. It was the most beautiful moment for Nalini.

It had been months since Satya had really laughed and seemed so happy and healthy.

It was the best allegory that her daughter had ever read and something she genuinely loved.

The following week when they made their routine visit to the doctor, he was pleased with the progress and was very optimistic about her complete recovery.

That night after she had finished with Tishani Doshi's 'Pleasure Seekers', she switched off the light before leaving the room, kissed Satya's forehead and whispered, "God bless my darling," see you in the morning.

6

The Night That Changed My Life

The bus was expected to leave at 9.30 in the night from *Coimbatore* for my cousin's marriage in *Trichy*. I was very excited.

"Priya stop moping around and get the luggage in the bus please," screamed my mother.

Ah! Always being told what to do was irking me now. Why should I do all the work? Why can't my brother do the work? He sits around holding a book reading all the time. He would always be the good guy and I am the black sheep. For once, I would love to swap places with him! Never mind, I would surely have a fantastic time tomorrow and Prasanth can read his book, while I will surely enjoy at the wedding. Those thoughts lasted till I got into the bus and settled down.

Preeti would surely look beautiful, what with all the new saris, jewellery and beauty parlour treatment, etc. The glow her skin has acquired would surely make any girl feel jealous. Well it doesn't matter I will wear my best *lehenga* and choli dress and everybody would be surprised and awestruck. As I thought about this, I noticed that Uncle Raghu was looking all smug and comfortable but thankfully, he left the seat next to mine. I really don't want his snoring to disturb me the entire night.

Just as the bus was completely packed and we were all set to go, a very handsome, young man entered.

He carried a long backpack which some what looked as if he was carrying a guitar or maybe a violin. Well, my heart skipped a beat when he promptly took the seat next to mine. My mother glanced from her side on the opposite seat but didn't really seem to mind. He must be one of the boy's side relatives. Just then the bus started and everyone in the bus chanted, *'Sri Ganeshayah Namah'* in unison.

The bus had just about turned from Ramnagar when my little cousin, Ashok came running to me and asked whether he could sit on my lap.

"Oops sorry, you can sit on my lap if you want," said the man sitting next to me and my young cousin looked at the young man and told him, "I don't know who you are and my mom tells me that I should not talk to strangers."

"That is good but you do know me now. My name is Anirudh and I am your cousin too!"

"*Akka*, do you mind if I sit on *Anna*'s lap?" Asked Ashok,

"Sure dear just don't disturb him." I answered, amused.

"No problems, he can sit as long as he wants," said the handsome hunk and my heart just missed another beat.

He must have seen me blush but did not show it. Why am I complaining?

He had the most enamouring smile that I had ever seen.

"*Anna* what do you have in your bag," asked Ashok innocently noticing the huge long bag that was lying on the bus floor.

As the bus lurched, I almost fell into his arms and he had to steady himself from falling and holding Ashok which he somehow managed. "It's nothing, only my guitar. Do you want to listen if I play it now?"

There was some murmur from the oldies in the front seat but my mother encouraged him and said, "It's okay, play something from the old Tamil songs and we will all sleep peacefully." My father mumbled something; almost like don't disturb me now. I am already asleep.

My mother clamped up after that. I knew that she was dying to know who he was and how was he related to the family, but maybe tomorrow, when they reached Trichy they can scrutinise the young man about his lineage. As of now, all of them wanted to sleep at least for some time.

He took out the guitar from the huge bag, there was something else there but in the dim bus light, I could not make out what it was and I didn't want to seem curious.

What would he think of me?

He adjusted the guitar in such a way that I could sit comfortably without getting disturbed, but he turned the other way and moved Ashok to my lap. The song that he played was an old MGR hit film song from the 70's and he played it beautifully. I closed my eyes and simply lost myself to the music. It was the third song that he must have played when I noticed that Ashok too had slept off.

I saw Anirudh quietly keep the guitar inside and he must have bent towards me since I felt his moist breath close to me but when I opened my eyes, he was looking the other way. I must have slept off and as I was gliding effortlessly into the world of soft soothing dreams since I was steadily rocked by the rhythmic movement of the bus, I lost count of time. A big jolt woke me and I almost dropped Ashok from my lap.

Anirudh was not there and it was almost pitch dark except the occasional light on the highway eating joints which were open round the clock for bus and truck drivers. I moved slightly from my seat to check out on Anirudh's whereabouts when I saw him bending over my aunt, two seats in the front. My curiosity got the better of me and I got up and made Ashok comfortable in Anirudh's seat. I wish I had not done that because what I noticed would be etched in my mind forever. Anirudh was removing my aunt's necklace and was putting it in his bag which was now lying near his feet.

The guitar was nowhere to be seen but what I saw in the bag was a huge dagger and a gun. I did not know what make the gun was, maybe Prasanth would be able to rattle the names and make of the weapon that lay before me, but as for me, I was just far too stunned to move. My father woke up suddenly. It was possible that the silence woke him or my prayer, I would never know.

"Hey! What are you doing?" and at this booming bombast almost all of the bus stirred and suddenly my mother screamed.

She touched her neck and her necklace was missing. I felt cheated and horrified. My dream had just been shattered. Anirudh had the ruthless look in his eyes, was this same soft eyes that had looked at me admiringly and lovingly? What a fool I have been!

In a flash, Anirudh picked up Ashok in one hand and in the other, he held a gun which was big but not heavy. It had a nozzle like fitting in its front, and in a voice most menacing ordered everyone to sit quietly.

"Hey, you beautiful, just get up from there and come here," he was ordering me! I went as if in a trance.

He told me to collect every bit of jewellery that was in and around the bus. I started doing what he said because he held Ashok as a captive and I knew that one wrong move and he would hurt Ashok.

The bus driver was oblivious of the commotion inside the bus, since it was divided by a door and he could not hear anything.

When I picked up the last bit of jewellery from my crying grandmother, I went to him, he looked as if he was about to say something in my ears,

"Why do you need that beautiful" and I felt a sharp tear around my neck as he effortlessly pulled my chain away. I felt shorn of everything at that moment.

He knocked on the door of the driver's cabin and told him sweetly that he needed to stop since he urgently required to relieve himself.

Just as the bus slowed, he handed Ashok in a jiffy into my unsuspecting arms and from the other pulled the bag that I carried. The door opened and he disappeared. The driver waited but the commotion that accosted him from the inmates made him jump from the bus in search of the missing miscreant.

Fifteen minutes later, they could not trace him. It was like the night had engulfed him.

The bus was abuzz with noise and I moved in a daze to my seat, buried my head in my hands and cried.

Nobody noticed me as each one was discussing and crying and screaming and lamenting as if they had lost a loved one. The happy and gay marriage trip was stripped of all its resplendent glory and left naked and humbled. All of the sixteen travellers had the most humiliating experience of their lives. Gone was the arrogance of money and matter. A young strapling of a man had sheared them of all their self-esteem.

No one knew who he was and I was sure they would never be able to find out either. The nocturnal night had played its last shenanigans and there was no turning back.

My mother had lost her *Mangalsutra* and her necklace, my father was thankful that the boy did not shoot him; my aunt was relieved that Ashok was alright. My grandmother had lost only a thin chain.

Each one lamented on the loss and thanked God that their life was spared. As for me, I had lost something most precious, I had lost myself to the piper's music and my heart to his soul.

7

The Green Grass

Balaji was excited when he arrived home.

"We are going to KL." "What's KL," asked Ramani.

"Oh! So it's finalised?" Sunandha asked incredulously.

"Yes its official, we are all going to Kaula Lumpur in March and will live there for a year or so, it should not matter since it would be fun, right?"

Wow! What thrilling news, Sunandha thought. Imagine how their relatives would react. The fun of living in a foreign country, coming back to India after a year and sharing their wonderful experience and even Ramya and Ramani can talk about their life there in KL!

Plans were afloat to shift. Both Balaji and Sunandha had a daunting task ahead of them. They had to sell a lot of their personal things from their two-bedroom flat at Mayur Vihar in Delhi and had decided to keep most of their remaining things in one room, locked of course and then give the other room, kitchen for rent. Fate seemed to be smiling at them and so without much effort, things just fell in place. Their cousin, who had recently taken a job in NOIDA, agreed to take the room on rent, and there was nothing to worry since he was family and none of their precious property would be lost.

After all, one cannot trust everyone these days!

Life was a confusion in KL for some time. Both Ramya and Ramani got admission in an Indian school, and were well settling down since all others were Indians too. There was this wonderful camaraderie amongst the Indians and soon Sunandha too fell into the life of living abroad. Their apartment was on the twenty first floor, quite intimidating at first, but soon they got used to the strict rules of making less noise and doing all the household chores almost by themselves, since getting any help was way off their budget. Sunandha found the afternoon boring, so she took to swimming in the pool and realised that it was indeed an invigorating exercise and in about a month's time, she had knocked off about fifteen pounds and felt fresh and agile.

Balaji had to find ways to occupy the family on weekends and in due course, made friends with his Indian colleagues. They had their small group of pot lunch in the weekends to follow. Sunandha looked forward to her annual trip to India, where she could talk about her absolutely wonderful life that she led in KL and how she would gush about the neatness and cleanliness of the city and the rules that everyone followed strictly.

She believed that she was more Indian than an Indian in India and therefore, religiously did her *puja* and wore all the beautiful silk saris and jewels that she possessed. She could wear all of them to their meetings and kitty parties. In fact, she would discuss with her friends in KL about how it was impossible to wear jewellery in India, since it was unsafe. Almost always after the party would get over, her friends would pitch in to take the leftovers to their house and sometimes, some of them stayed back to help cleaning the plates and clearing the table. Sunandha would otherwise find it a drudgery of having to clean everything on her own. Balaji being the typical Indian husband would not move a muscle to help her but of late, Sunandha had seen a change in him. He was getting up from his seat to see to it that the work was done and kitchen cleared before they went to bed.

Sunandha would wait for the night since mobile rates were high. When the trunk rates were less and then place a call to her mother and talk for some time updating them about the fantastic parties that she was attending. Sometimes, she would not even realise that she had taken well into their sleeping time and that they were really bored of listening.

During those days Sunandha would seldom realise that because she was desperate and wanted to share her foreign experience with her people in India and sometimes would even say in all jocularity that they should visit them at KL. It would be very expensive to entertain guests at home of course, but there was no harm in suggesting, was there? Unlike India, where anyone can come and live and it would hardly bend the budget, without servants it would be most difficult at KL, but what else could she do? Sunandha would fervently want her family to see how well she was living.

Balaji too would wait for his visit to India, where he would meet his college friends and other relatives and talk for hours about the Malaysian islands and the homogeneous life that the Chinese, Malaysians and the Tamils, who lived there, led. What a country! But the year was about to end and with a heavy heart; the couple anticipated their return to India. How can they go back? Wouldn't it be difficult to adjust to the traffic, the teeming population, the dirt and garbage, the noise pollution and the general lack of civic sense in Indians?

They waited with trepidation.

It was around March when the news came and really what news! Balaji rushed home from work and this time, Sunandha was too stunned to react.

They were expected to go to the United States of America, the land of opportunities and nothing less.

The children, of course were indifferent; they didn't care one way or the other. They would miss their friends of course. Ramya was more reluctant. She was entering her teens and did not want to lose her classmates and the Indian friends whom she was really close to, but Ramani didn't care anyways.

"Wait till I tell Amma and Appa, " Sunandha exploded.

And that night was the most celebrated night of their life. Unfortunately, Sunandha's father was unwell and died in his sleep in the following month. Tragedy struck again, when her mother too passed away six months later. Sunandha was on one hand busy and confused about her shift to Boston and on the other, the loss of her parents. Money was tight too. She had to make two trips within six months, which turned out to be the most unexpected pressure on their frugal budget.

A year later, when they were told that they could stay in the United States for further two years, both Balaji and Sunandha felt relieved. They could now make new friends, Indians, of course. Ramya was becoming quite difficult to handle, her teens, adolescent crushes and her lack of initiatives to make friends. Sunandha had her hands full.

She was in her words, 'quite freaked out' by the American lifestyle.

Sunandha would desperately hunt for an Indian face in the market or any shopping that she ventured. Her desperation to meet Indians made her rather grumpy at home. She would often find herself alone and lonely and with the twelve hour difference between India and the United States, she could hardly get enough time to talk to her brother Anand or sister-in-law, Uma. Somehow according to Sunandha, Uma had risen to the occasion and had become her close friend after the painful time when she lost her parents. Life for Sunandha had become a drudgery in the U.S. She would just do her housework and wait for the kids and Balaji to return home at the end of the day. He would return after a thirty-mile drive and would be irritable and tired. She could have looked for a job, but somehow, it never really materialised. Maybe, she lacked the initiative, confidence and the drive to venture into the new world.

Those days she would consider her life in India, where at least she could ask the servants to get her provisions, vegetables and short eats available anywhere and everywhere.

She would feel bored of eating the same kind of food and would dearly miss the hot *samosas* and *kachoris* that were available at Mayur Vihar, and sign in sheer nostalgia.

Time is a wonderful tool and it took them all under its ambivalent wings and like KL, they made their own group of Indian friends. Thus, life became a routine with parties at their Indian friends' houses. That was when Sunandha had taken refuge with Yoga and would attend classes at her friend's house. Meditation gave her the peace of mind that she craved for so desperately. Her loneliness was eating into her and she was unable to find a reason for it. Her friends said maybe homesickness, but wasn't this the life that she always wanted, so why was she feeling homesick?

When her friends suggested a psychiatrist, Sunandha then realised that she had to go home. So Balaji, who was also suffering the same pangs gladly agreed to make his trip to India and very soon preparation went underway to procure tickets, presents and gifts for friends and relatives. It was now close to five years since they had moved away from India and Sunandha's heart beat faster when the plane landed at the IGI airport at New Delhi. Now it was called T3 and looked so amazing that for a moment, she felt that she was back in the States!

'Anna' and Uma with Radhika had come to the airport to pick them up. The new Honda City with a smart driver who stood to attention and picked up their luggage without much effort made her feel warm, happy, proud and jealous at the same time.

Just as Sunandha was about to say something about the driver and the car, her attention was diverted by her admiration of the scenic beauty of Delhi with the metro running regularly and the innumerable flyovers and expressways transported her back to the United States.

The small apartment that her brother had acquired after the death of their parents was not small at all! It had three bedrooms with attached bath, a Jacuzzi and a modular kitchen. Sunandha was very impressed. The cook was waiting for them with two *sabzi,* one made of cottage cheese and the other was a seasonal cauliflower, potato, carrot and green peas.

The *rotis* that followed made Sunandha feel so comforted that she just called it a day, what with the jet lag and fatigue with such good hot food.

The following morning after a cup of hot filter coffee, Balaji announced that he would go to meet his friends and may or may not be back for dinner. He picked up the sprays and deodorants that he had bought for his friends and went his way.

Ramya was mighty thrilled. She and Radhika shared a good number of friends in their facebook profile and got down to talking about their common friends.

Ramya had been rather reluctant to come, but she had been advised by Sunandha that if she touches any elderly person's feet they would bless her and give her Indian rupees that she can collect, keep and even show off to her American friends! Since Radhika was a year younger to Ramya, it was not difficult for the two young teenagers to hit it off big time.

That morning, Ramya and Radhika decided to check out the local malls which had mushroomed around the colony and as she stepped outside, she met Mr. Sharma, the neighbour and like a diver ready for a jump from the diving ramp, Ramya plunged at Mr. Sharma's feet but the way he moved away from her made Ramya recoil, as if electrified.

Mr. Sharma was scandalised and told her that young girls should not touch anybody's feet since they were considered goddesses themselves.

Ramani enjoyed himself since he was given the wholesome control on the PS 3 that was there for him to indulge. He just about had a blast and was disturbed only when he was called for hot Tiffin or sumptuous lunch. Sunandha was having the time of her life, earlier when she would come to India, her mother would take care of every need of hers, but now Uma was doing a great job too with her array of servants and hospitality.

Something was nagging her now.

What would she do if her brother's family decided to pay them a visit? Can she provide the same kind of hospitality?

"Sunandha care for a cappuccino," Uma asked breaking Sunandha's reverie.

"Oh! By the way, I have brought you a bag, care to check it out? "Thanks Sunandha," Uma said without even reacting to the object she held.

She quickly went to her cupboard and came back with another bag similar to what Sunandha was holding.

"Here check this out!" And she showed her a duplicate, Louis Vitton bag.

Uma held her bag proudly and suddenly Sunandha felt small. Not to be outdone Sunandha said,

"I have some shades of lipstick that you would simply love Uma". I just as Sunandha brought out the Revlon collection of different shades, Uma too had another set with her.

This time Sunandha could not take it anymore. She just excused herself after asking Uma how she had brought the new set in India because the combination of her colours was quite recent in the United States.

It seemed that all these shades were available in the great malls, where new showrooms had come up and almost all the products that were available anywhere in the world were also available in India.

This information was somehow too much for Sunandha, who just about called it a day, while complaining about her headache. Balaji came back a little later, kind of frustrated himself. His friends were either busy or unavailable to meet him and the one friend, who did come for a coffee had far too many things going for him to even listen to Balaji's foreign conquest.

Well it was too much really, he could not bear this insolence. Earlier, when he would come to India, his friends would eagerly wait for his gifts and would fight over, who would call the family for lunch or dinner.

Balaji prided about his great Indian circle of friends to his American counterparts and now it seemed that he hardly had any stories to tell except that India has almost everything available and the middle class could afford all that they prided in possessing in the United States. Somehow, he and Sunandha had overlooked the fact that everything would change and not just them, whom he thought had the right to a better life, it was but natural and imperative that better life is what everyone craved and wanted and eventually got. This change was unacceptable for him.

But India or Indians were no less, and with intelligence and vision, they had climbed the ladder of success, just as everyone else. Change was a global phenomenon, and it was happening in India pretty fast.

Somehow, the stay did not remain the same for the couple and after a cursory visit to temples etc; it was decidedly time to call it quits. The days just seemed to pass after that and then it was time to go back.

Sunandha recalled about the times when her parents were alive and whenever, she would come to India, Uma would be wearing a sari and serving food to all of them. Now with the smart haircut and fitting Levis jeans and Mark and Spencer T-shirts, she looked so hip that Sunandha herself felt that she needed to revamp her wardrobe! Uma had really changed.

Ramya had really been confused with the Sharma episode and it had taken a day for Sunandha to clear the confusion about touching feet of the elders for girls in south India and the stark opposite of it in the northern part of India. It seemed that

Ramani was the only one who was without any bitter incident added to his experience.

The day they boarded the plane for the United States, Sunandha and Balaji realised for the first time that things were different. India has changed and people have accepted all the changes well in their stride.

And when the plane took off from T3, Sunandha realised and felt perhaps for the first time that they didn't belong anywhere anymore and home was now the United States and yes, *the grass is definitely not greener on the other side.*

8

Ambujam Mami

Ammu was very young, she really doesn't remember how young she was when she got married. She probably remembers herself only after her marriage. Well, she still remembers her grandmother who taught her to cook when she was a young girl, maybe, twelve or thirteen years old. Her own mother, Ammu sighs and remembers, was always busy taking care of her brothers and sisters. It would seem that she was pregnant almost all the years that she had known her. Ammu was proud of the fact that apart from two of her younger brothers, her seven siblings were alive and doing very well. Amma would tell her to take care of her brothers and sisters, while she rested in the other room. Often she would become tired and Ammu would lovingly bathe and feed her brothers and sisters. She was the eldest and then her sister and their three brothers and then her two sisters and then the youngest brother, who was more like her own son.

"*Akka* come here please," was often the call and she would rush to them and would do all the needful, whether it was night or day.

Amma died when Ammu was only fourteen leaving her to take care of everyone in the house. Grandmother too was very old and tired, although everyone around pitied her for being so young and responsible, Ammu never really felt any remorse.

She loved cooking and every day she would buy vegetables for the next day and decide on the day's paltry menu. Sometimes *Appa* could only give her enough money for one vegetable and tell her before he went to work that he could give her only a rupee to buy whatever she wanted. Ammu never felt sorry or sad, she just knew what she could buy with that money and everyday, she was able to feed them with hot food twice a day. Bananas were always there if one felt hungry, wasn't it?

Her memory is hazy now and when little Karthik prodded her further to tell her stories, she told him "I am tired *kanna*, tomorrow *Patti* will tell you the story of your father's childhood now let me sleep."

When Ramki returned home, he saw his mother tiredly sleeping on the floor. He felt a pang of love for her. She would never sleep on the cot, force of habit, he thought.

Ammu was not having the same enthusiasm and energy like before, he recalled yet when she woke up at the break of dawn she was up and about as if nothing else mattered than the beautiful day ahead.

Ammu was married to Sitaraman when she was seventeen because by then, Rajam, her younger sister was able to take care of her siblings and Sitaraman seemed like an eligible choice for her at that time.

Sitaraman was twenty-nine and was working at a small rice godown as a clerk and was paid twenty rupees every month. The age difference was hardly a consideration for such an eligible man and in the April of the year when Ammu turned seventeen, she found herself married and ushered into a life that was more than just cooking and taking care of her siblings.

She now had to do her wifely duties and also cook, clean the house, take care of her in-laws, her brother-in-law, sister-in-law and all the relatives, who would constantly drop in at any time of the day. She being the first daughter-in-law was expected to be alert, friendly and hospitable at the same time. Maybe it is that training that made her a happy person all the time.

Ammu delivered Ramki when she was nineteen years old and Sushila was born when she turned twenty two. Now she was a mother apart from all the other roles that she played. Ammu's friendly nature made her a considerate neighbour and often she would be helping her neighbours in the *Agraharam* where she lived in a small house which shared walls with her neighbours on either side. Life was pleasantly going on but when Ramki was only ten years old, Sitaraman died unexpectedly due to a heart attack.

Now it all fell on Ammu's tender shoulders to support her family. Her brother-in-law, Shankar was just in his intermediate and with the help of some relatives in Delhi, he went to look for a job but the others were dependent on her. No property or land to back them up left the family to fend for themselves. It was Aruna from the next house, who suggested that Ammu should make *Murruku* rice based savouries prepared in bulk and sold in the nearby condiment store. Ammu was promised five rupees for twenty packets that she could make and give and if there was a regular clientele, then more was promised.

Ammu's pickles were another delectable delicacy that she was known for and in three months time, Ammu's pickles found a market too.

Ammu would get up at four thirty in the morning and would sweep the entrance of the house, and decorate it with *kolam.* Then she would clean the house and get to cooking brunch.

The idea of breakfast never existed and almost everyone ate brunch (that was breakfast and lunch together). Ammu would then set to prepare her pickles like mango, lime, tender mangoes and even gooseberries which she would buy in the evening at the market at Luz corner and equipped with the materials, she would set to the task of pickling them and then bottling them in jars provided by the condiment store. When her mother-in-law passed away, Ammu was left without any company to help her in her chores of cutting and cooking.

Ammu had seen the country through its independence struggle and she was part of a struggle too! She had mouths to feed didn't she without help or assistance and had to struggle to survive? As the years rolled by, Ammu's pickles became famous and popular in and around Mylapore, where she had been living for almost twenty-five years.

Ramki was now working in an office at Mount Road and would travel everyday by train and walk the distance from there. He would carry his mother's homemade food in a *Tiffin* carrier and his friends would eagerly look forward to his lunch spread of one *Porial*, *Kootu* and *Sambar* with rice in a separate box. She would have tied a banana leaf along with the lunch so when Ramki would sit down to have his lunch, it would be a literal feast. Often, she would send some sweets too. Ammu's *Mysore pak* was a sure shot and once Ramki's boss had tasted it and had become an instant fan.

As Ramki grew in his post and position, it was time for them to shift to a bigger house at Anna Nagar. Although Ammu was happy and pleased at her son's growth, she dreaded the idea of shifting to a new house.

Sushila's marriage was a grand affair and Ammu wore her silk sari with style. She had gone to Pondy bazaar to buy it and when it was time for her to shift to the new house at Anna Nagar, it was probably the only time when she would have felt a deep foreboding. Ammu's 'Pal Payasam' won her the new friends in the new house at Anna Nagar and as usual, Ammu's time was occupied with preparing pickles, *Papadam*, *Murruku* and other savouries that she was known to make perfectly. Ramki had forbidden her to sell any more products but he was unable to stop the neighbours rush to his house at all time of the day and sometimes even at night.

Ammu's medicinal concoction that she prepared for a lactating mother was another popular hit. "*Mami* please prepare the medicine for my cousin at Delhi," the neighbourhood ladies would ask and Ammu would get to work.

Ramki's marriage to Lakshmi brought the much awaited company in the kitchen that Ammu really needed and together they would get down to preparing the most delectable lunch that the whole neighbourhood had ever tasted.

The birth of little Karthik was a wonderful moment for Ammu and she would take it upon herself to take care of him all day, every day. Lakshmi would fondly complain saying, "Amma you are pampering him."

Ammu would smile and say, "as long as I live, let me take care of him," and this would quieten her for some time.

Lakshmi would wonder what she would do without her loving mother-in-law, who had suffered enough hardship in life and had never complained even once.

She would discuss with her family members telling them how she admired her mother-in-law for her spirit and her determination and patience.

Ammu died in her sleep peacefully and somehow, her story about Ramki's childhood would remain untold and little

Karthik may never be able to know or understand the life that his grandmother had led.

Her life story which was an example to many ladies would be often discussed among the families of Anna Nagar and Mylapore in Chennai even today.

9

Fit for a Queen

The afternoon was hot, but never mind, the kitty usually holds some cool promises. Sujatha reflected pensively. She was getting dressed to go to Revathi's house since she was hosting the kitty party this time. The four friends had decided that they really did not want any new members for the sake of money. What is the need when all they wanted to was to chill out together so that they could discuss and gossip about their lives and also make some money in the bargain! Sujatha pondered over these, while she chose a white sari with sequins, the theme for the day's party was peace. The thoughts that went through her mind may not have been all peaceful but never mind, at least the sari should reflect otherwise.

Revathi, on the other hand was frantic that nothing really was ready for the party. She remembered how her husband Raghu had sniggered about her elaborate preparations.

His exact words were, "why so much fuss?" and Revathi had literally blown a fuse. He doesn't understand. She had to make time from her work and schedule everything on a Saturday which happens to be an off day from her work at the 'Jumanji solutions' where she was employed as a personal secretary.

Agreed that it was not much of a name or a position or place to work but at least she was not a housewife like Sujatha!

How is he ever going to understand that she had to make an impression on Sujatha and others that even when she is working, she can put up a spread fit for a queen!

Somewhere else Supriya pondered how she was going to manage her little Suresh during the time she was gone for the kitty. Should she take him with her? Maybe not! He would just be in the way. Finally, she decided that she would leave him at her neighbour's house with his friend, Rishabh. Well that is settled, but oh God! What about the white sari that she had not bothered to procure? Never mind maybe Rita, Rishabh's mother can help her out. After all, it was a matter of hot *Iddlys* and *Sambar* for the Sunday. She was a schoolteacher and maybe, she did not earn as much as her friends, surely that did not make her less appealing, so what if she did'nt have money like her friends, she definitely planned to compensate with her looks!

Ambika had a different worry altogether. Her elderly in-laws would need their coffee in the evening but why should she always worry about it all the time?

Can't her sister-in-law take care for one more day; after all she was a Chartered Accountant working as a consultant for link services. Yes! That is that then.

When Arun comes in the evening she would explain how it was important for her to attend the kitty and maybe, make his favourite *kheer* in the evening. Then probably he would not protest that Chandrika was doing all the work. Imagine the audacity of Chandrika to always complain that Ambika was never at home and all that but really! How much can a person do? Contribute to the family expenses and also do housework round the clock.

When the door bell rang, Revathi was giving finishing touches to the table and adjusting her white salwar suit that she had worn. So what if it was not a sari, it was surely white, wasn't it? Ambika breezed in followed by Sujatha looking skeptical and of course, the beautiful Supriya entered last! After the preliminary greetings and exchanges where almost no one really understood what the other was saying, a kind of calm descended, while they settled on the ample sofa that was new in Revathi's house. The smell of *Dosa* and *Chutney* wafted the nostrils and like magnets, they rushed towards the table.

No no! That is not done. What about the short eat and the warm 'garlic rasam' that Revathi had prepared as an appetizer.

Giggling, they settled down to the chiding and admonishing by Revathi and their appetites was almost placated by the *Rasam* and *Vadas*.

"What do you want to do? Should we play a game of *Tambola,"*asked Revathi having the kitty well under her control.

"No! Let's sort the money out of the way," said Sujatha not to be outdone. She was the housewife who knew how to do a kitty. "Ok agreed," Ambika said in a matter of fact tone.

Revathi collected her thirty thousand rupees and was content. The next kitty fell for Ambika, but instead of the happy expression, there was a frown.

"What is wrong," asked Supriya. "Nothing really. It would be difficult to organise the kitty at home, so maybe I should do it in a restaurant if you girls agree."

Revathi was quick to smirk, "why can't you do it at your lovely home?"

"No I can't, Chandrika won't help me in any way and my in-laws would object."

"That is not fair, why wouldn't she help?" Sujatha was quick to ask. "What can I say, nowadays, she has her tantrums. I am the elder of the daughters-in-law, yet she shows no respect.

I remember when I got married I had to bow down to almost everyone at home but now she refuses to do even the smallest favour and to think I do so much for the family!"

"The youngsters today think no end of themselves," added Supriya matter of factly.

In my school, there are new teachers who prance around the school with so much energy and enthusiasm that all the work and accolades seems to go their way, the management had the audacity to tell me that I should just teach because I am a good teacher and not to worry; there are others– more energetic ones to do my job. Tell me is that justified? I have worked so many years and there is no respect for seniority. These youngsters today work for consolidated salary and seem very happy doing so. Imagine!" Supriya concluded angrily.

Revathi was the next to lament, "In my office there is this young girl who has joined recently and she dances around the boss all day and seems happy doing every odd job. One day the boss told me to get him a hot cup of cafe latte and I refused.

"Am I some sort of peon or servant that I do such menial jobs? But imagine this young thing goes by the name of Monica jumps at the opportunity and comes back happy and cheerful.

The boss is thrilled with her. All my years of service, hard work, staybacks and heart wrenching work overlooking the family has all gone waste over a cup of coffee. Now if I start getting him the coffee what would happen to my self-esteem?"

It was a woeful cry that escaped Revathi's lips and it seemed as if she would burst into tears.

All the exertion of the day over and above living with this fact that she was almost redundant in the office made her weak.

Sujatha watched her friends and realised that being a housewife she has been hearing people just shrug at her and say, 'Oh so you are just a housewife' and always feel a pang of jealousy against her friends, who would wear beautiful clothes and go off to office, while she stayed at home taking care of her beautiful and tastefully decorated house which she had created painstakingly picking and choosing each item with love and care. Now her friends seemed somewhat frail and weak, while she was comfortable! Imagine it had taken her so many years to realise that working women had to handle a lot. Their homes, families, relatives and friends above all, take care of themselves because they had to do multiple tasks almost every day. They were all the modern day Goddess *Kali* and each possessed more arms than needed.

A sudden thought flashed and Sujatha literally jumped in her seat. "Why don't we all start a business, we can open a boutique or a coffee shop or a book store cum coffee shop and take care of it?"

She looked triumphantly at her three friends expecting immediate response, but she met with quizzical gaze from all of them.

"What?" Shouted Ambika, "And what may I ask I should do?" "Oh no problem, you can take care of the accounts". Sujatha said non-chalantly.

They all burst out laughing. It was after the much anticipated lunch, while they settled once again with a hot cup of coffee, that the subject was browsed upon once again.

"So what do you think, should we do it?" Sujatha picked up from where she had left off.

Good idea but how can we leave our jobs; we have worked for so many years, wailed Revathi plaintively.

"I will take care of the nitty gritty", volunteered Sujatha once again. "Maybe it's not such a bad idea", Supriya agreed. She had been a teacher for a long time and she was disillusioned with the system. She was not cut out for bigger things, it seemed and starting one's own business may not be such a bad idea. She could leave the job and take care of the books section of the shop. After all, she was an avid book reader.

While she contemplated gleefully, the others too pondered on similar thoughts. Revathi knew that it wouldn't be easy to leave the comfort zone of her air-conditioned office and work in a coffee shop. The question that bothered her most was what was she expected to do there? Not selling coffee I hope, she prayed fervently and soon her fears were put to rest.

"Revathi you can do the data entry in the office, we would create for you."

And Ambika you must take care of the accounts and I will take care of the coffee and confectioneries and Supriya you can surely take care of the books?"

"Wow someone has done serious homework today, since when have you been planning this Sujatha?" asked Ambika curiously. "Oh it's nothing, I have been considering business ventures all this while and today when I heard you girls cribbing about your work, it became easier. I never knew that you were all beset with so many issues in the workplace. Let me taste the world of women entrepreneurship!"

Let's celebrate the idea with a round of good Tetley tea, suggested Revathi who was feeling that maybe, she had not been a good host and once again, Sujatha, the homemaker was taking the centrestage!

"Yes, why not?" Everyone chorused in unison, breaking into her reverie.

"Now let's discuss the place where we should buy and how we should start." Sujatha started once again.

The phone from Ambika's purse rang loud and Ambika literally jumped out of her skin, picking up her phone, She answered excitedly and everyone waited for her to finish.

"Oh but I have to go, my mother-in-law is not feeling well and Chandrika has thrown in the towel," saying Ambika hugged everyone and bid a quick adieu.

Supriya quickly checked whether Suresh was all right and then she was told that he had fallen down in the bathroom and was crying for her. Supriya made a quick exit too leaving Sujatha and Revathi to sort it out. "Well, what should we do?" Asked Revathi wanting Sujatha also to leave since she had enough cleaning to do and preparing for the following day and its related work.

Sujatha took the cue and beat a hasty retreat. Maybe, they can discuss it in the next kitty at Ambika's place and why not, thought Sujatha, she did have lots of time to do so!

10

No Stones Upturned

"Oh! So you are Narayanan and not Narayan", Raghav spoke impetuously.

"Well! What's in a name", I said smiling at his belligerence.

After all, this was a common enough incident in my career... definitely not for the first time. I had just joined the school as an English teacher and I knew that it would be a struggle to survive. I strongly believed that I would love to throttle and shoot the person who said, 'teaching was easy'.

"Oh! So you are Narayanan Subramanian Sir, Why? Isn't it a South Indian name"?

The class sniggered and my blood boiled. I cursed the day when my father decided to address me with such a long name. Why can't it be something short and sweet like Ajay or Sunil?

When I got out of the class, I was summoned by the principal.

"Mr. Narayan I am sure you are getting to know your class, in our school we have very high standards of academic excellence and our teachers need to work hard to improve the student's behaviour and every aspect of personality development. Our teachers are also counselors rolled into one."

The smile which followed was dismissive and as I turned to leave the vice-principal who had hitherto kept quiet said,

"Mr. Narayan you can collect your job confirmation slip from the office."

My sister's house was in the same area as my school at 'Arera colony', a posh locality in Bhopal and as I went home, I was greeted by my twelve-year old nephew, Sairam who grinned at me mischievously and said, "So how was your day?"

"Ok I guess", I said and walked inside. My sister was waiting for me and gave me a cup of filter coffee.

After my mother's death the previous year, I had looked up to Sailakshmi more and more for emotional support. She reminded me of my mother so much when she stood there with the coffee that my voice choked but I smiled and thanked her for the coffee. My brother-in-law worked for a multi-national company and was merely tolerant of my presence. I knew this because I was after all a school teacher and not an executive like him earning in lakhs. I have great respect for my profession. I know that somewhere out there was this one student who was not merely listening to me but imbibing each word that I said as the most important learning lesson.

I am a teetotaler and I believe that teachers need to set fine examples for their students and many a time, I would land up in a major argument with my friends and family.

My brother-in-law avoided me primarily for this reason but I would often look for sympathy and would make up as a sob story stating that he hated me because I am just a school teacher.

My father too was not appreciative of the fact that I earned so little yet he respected the profession I had chosen.

Much as he wanted me to turn out to be an engineer or a doctor, I performed mediocre at school and therefore became incompetent to join any reputed institutions for professional courses. When I did my B.ed after my post graduation, I had become an object of mockery but I knew I would enjoy teaching because maybe that is what I had always wanted to do. Teaching according to many was after all a woman's domain because a man cannot manage the economics of a family life without a good handsome salary.

Maybe, I should supplement my salary by giving some tuitions, I contemplated.

My mother had wanted me to get married but with the salary I earned, I knew that no sane man would give his daughter in marriage to me. I couldn't afford any luxuries, I knew that.

As I washed my feet and changed into my customary *kurta* and *pajama* for the night, my sister asked me whether I could help Sai with his homework. I entered his room after knocking, and was surprised to see him busy with his work.

My sister had definitely done her homework well. Sai was turning out to be a hardworking diligent young man. Wish I had been this hard working, maybe, I would have been an executive of a multinational, I sighed.

"*Mama*, Can you teach me the figures of speech? I am supposed to know them by tomorrow and none of them make any sense to me."

"Let me see," I said and promised to come back to him in an hour's time with everything well explained.

I had an idea. One hour later, I entered his room again with a piece of paper. "What is it?" He asked, then he read it aloud.

Word smithy

Simple Simon smiled in silent stupor
While the haughty hero hammered the hideous hunter
Alliteration is it? Asked the able gable.
Maybe an oxymoron ventured, the clearly confused
Like a metaphor suggested the smiling simile
No, no an imagery volunteered the voluble verb
Stop this utter nonsense said the eulogizing euphemism
If only this is true said the clashing clause
Hark! Ahem! Said the intelligent interjector
You are all confused said the nebulous noun
It's either common, or proper seldom abstract I presume
The adorable adjective sniggered pretentiously
But, even if, although said the conniving conjunction
Either ways it means the same exploded the transformer
Better word watched patiently and said benignly
Friends in the word smithy figure and parts smelts and melts
And form words of wisdom and intent
Opulent should be your form and sound
That your success should be lofty and resound.
So Take your beautiful form and go out into the world
And mould and smould your presence to young and old!
So saying better word closed the shop
Promising to unleash wordy wise worthy to the world
For posterity to remember and recount.

I looked at him triumphantly but he just dropped the paper and said, "What *Mama,* you could have given some examples. Now I am confused, you have mentioned both figures and parts. I need to write only about figures," he grumbled.

I picked up the paper and just then my sister appeared and took the paper from me, as she read it her eyes lighted up and she smiled and said, "You haven't lost your touch, I see," and I smiled at our little joke.

I would often help her with her writings and many a times, she had been appreciated for my efforts while she was in college. She knew I enjoyed writing poetry and often she had suggested that I should get them printed. I sighed, who would want to read the ramblings of a confirmed recluse? A subtitle I had given to myself and sadly picked the paper from her hand.

"Sai where is my coffee," came the voice of my *B-I-L* from the entrance and Sai ran to greet him. My father who had passed away when I was doing my post-graduation was a *Sai Baba bhakth* and had named my sister Sailakshmi and had insisted that his grandson should be called Sairam. Had there been a granddaughter he would have named her 'Saikeerthana' I am sure! My own story is well-known anyways. All this was often confusing, but I was told that the number of times we called out their names, as many times, we invoked God and thereby, earned more God's blessings.

I helped Sairam to finish his homework and then went to meet Ram short for Ramamurthy, my brother in law and talked about this and that and after dinner took a book to bed.

I am an avid book reader and had often extolled the virtues of book reading to the class, and the response was often lukewarm and tepid.

They would either yawn or make faces. Who wanted to read now that Google and Wikipedia was just a push button away?

While I pondered over *Finkler's Question* sleep came quietly and I slept restfully.

The next morning when I entered school, it was almost a repeat of the previous day, but my colleagues at Bhopal seemed friendlier than my friends at Coimbatore where I had worked earlier.

Mr. Sharma welcomed me to the staff room with a grin and asked, "so how is Bhopal treating you?" And I grinned back and said, "Good' very good so far!"

The classes were now getting somewhat familiar. Initially there was some sniggering, giggling and some sharp comments too. Soon this became a routine. I have been teaching for some years now. It was a month before I could cut the ice and get to know them. Children are children, so eventually, they became my friends.

They enjoyed my classes since I was able to show them my love and passion for the language and taught with panache. It wasn't an ordeal for them anymore because I taught in the most interactive way possible. I made up short poems of every word they said and after some time, they felt that writing poems was easy.

"Let me give you the first line, and then each one can add rhyming lines to it.

Is that okay?" I asked. "Yes Sir", they chorused. So it began.

Let's do some work

Not hang around like jokers

Create something ingenious

Out of our meager experience

Lofty ideas those are freaky and cheeky

That we are ready to rock and roll

Life is a ball just run and throw

That's the way to go I extolled!

Remember this is easy and the very best.

Oh! This is surely better than any test!

The whole class roared loudly and the happiness and comradeship was so infectious that I finally felt that I belonged.

'Good morning' would fondly become 'good morrow sir ' and it would please me immensely.

One day I was called to the principal's office and he told me that I was doing a great job and all the feedback that he had been receiving was positive and gave me a light warning that it was better to be slightly strict with the students, otherwise they would take me for a ride.

I was informed about a girl, Varsha in the eleventh grade who was showing exceptional interest for a boy of her class.

Apparently the only problem in this seemingly adolescent case was that the boy's father was the DCP of that area and it also seemed that the girl's other aspiring candidates for her affections had threatened the boy, Harsh of dire consequences if he did not stop his pursuit of Varsha.

Well now the DCP had decided to protect his son and also threatened the other boys who were pursuing Varsha and were ready to beat up his boy. I was wondering where I was fitting into the scheme of things.

'Mr. Narayan you need to counsel the girl and her parents about the situation.'

This was the crux of the problem. Now I had to become a counsellor and an educated concerned teacher. I was angry, here I was struggling to make two ends meet with the meager salary that the educational institutions threw at me time and again and instead of increasing my salary, they just were misusing my abilities for their ends.

Talk about 'in appreciation of good work, more work'.

The following week I went to Varsha's house and talked to her parents. Here was a delicate task.

Maybe the parents were not even aware of the girl's interests or her philandering attitude. And I was supposed to convince them and her about what? Honestly, I never thought I did well but maybe my worry for her showcased itself into genuine concern that the parents instantly understood the situation and promised to closely monitor every move of hers and her friends from then on.

Varsha did not take any of this well. Why would she? She was a teenager and she had every right to go out with her friends and pursue other such interests. Her harmless romance was becoming a cynosure of everybody's attention and Varsha seemed agitated and frustrated as I laid bare the facts.

Her being watched all the time was not a good idea and that too because her English teacher was saying so was an absolute hell for her!

I did all that I could to convince her that Harsh had issues of security and therefore it was a good idea to lay low for some time. When I reached home, I felt fatigued and angry, bitter and irritated. When Sairam came to ask some grammar doubts, I shooed him away.

The next day another problem had cropped up. Varsha had decided to take matters in her own hands and had planned to leave her house to some unknown destination without informing anyone!

Now I was in a bigger loop than before. The staff room seemed to have glaring eyes everywhere. None questioned me directly, but every eye seemed to ask what did I tell the girl? I was really angry. They ask a teacher like me to talk to a teenage girl then they blame me for it.

Talk about passing the buck! The school conveniently had put the blame on me by saying that I was the one to have counselled the girl. (English Spelling)

I decided to salvage the situation. Somehow the girl's welfare was paramount for me. I now approached the classmates and somehow they were more than willing to talk to me. They told me that she may have gone to her cousin's house, Vidisha. So complaining of a headache, taking half day from school. I took the next bus from Bhopal and with the address I had procured from her friends, I reached Varsha's uncle's place and as I entered the house, after nearly an hour of house hunting, I saw Varsha happily chatting.

I quickly apprised her of her situation and she immediately called up her parents who in turn called off the police. Everyone calmed down after that and waited for Varsha to return. When I reached home after uniting Varsha with her parents, I was tired but relieved.

At school the situation was different.

Teachers came and talked to me and said I had done the right thing of going to Vidisha alone to bring her back.

During the assembly, the principal talked about my contribution and thanked me for making the English language so much more interesting than what it was! Varsha's incident was not spoken openly, since it would bring disgrace on her.

The year rolled on without much happening (barring the debates, the annual day practice, the regular paper making, correction, and other such mundane official work) and then one day it seemed as if it was time to move on. I had applied at one of the premier institutions in Delhi and surprisingly, they had called me for an interview.

When I said bye to Sairam and my sister, I realised that I had learnt more than I had taught. No matter how educated you are, life always treats you like a student and every day, you learn a new lesson.

The school bade me a memorable farewell and I went richer with my experience and innumerable friends for life, who would remember me for teaching them about life. Maybe being a good human being was far more important than being just a good teacher or a professional earning lots of money.

Someday I might get married and maybe have a Sairam of my own; perhaps the only legacy that I would be able to leave for him would be a cornucopia of scruples and truckload of principles!

I realised that I had often told my students to think out of the box and not to remain a frog in the well and maybe, I had myself not been able to think 'out of the box'.

Teachers should not just preach but practice too.

Equipped with this lesson for life, I reached New Delhi with an open heart, mind and soul.

Glossary

The Gold Chain

Janawera: Sacred thread worn by a Brahmin

Thathan: Goldsmith so named in southern India

Kalpathy puzha: The Kalpathy River that flows in Palakkad in Kerala

Madarasi: Madarasi is an ethnic slur used for people of south India mostly by people of western, central and northern parts of the Indian subcontinent

Iddly: is a savoury cake of south India

Sambar: It is one of the most loved dishes in South Indian cuisine. It accompanies almost every meal

Marwari: An Indian ethnic group, that originates from the Rajasthan region of India

Rice sevai: This is an easy Indian food recipe that makes for a light, filling and quick fix breakfast meal

Revelation

Modus Operandi: Method of operating or functioning.

Vermillion: It is known as Kumkum or Sindoor in India

Parama Shiva Bhakth: A devotee of Lord Shiva.

Kaushy

Marar road: A place in Trissur, Kerala (India)

Linga: It is a representation of the Hindu deity used for worship in temples

Kolam: Design on the floor to decorate the entrance of the house in Southern India

Swami: South Indian name for God's and Goddess

Lalitha Sahasranama: The 1000 names of the divine mother 'Lalitha

Shiva Stuti: Invoking lord Shiva

Rasam: Indian soup, traditionally prepared using tamarind juice as a base

Vetriviza: A fictional name for a temple

Yakshi: Yakshi is the Yogini form of Padmavathi

Paal Payasam: A traditional dish in the Indian subcontinent, it is a rice pudding typically made by boiling rice with milk and sugar

The Night That Changed My Life

Coimbatore: City in Tamil Nadu, (India)

Langha: A traditional dress for girls in India

Sri Ganeshayah Namah: Invoking Lord Ganesha

Akka: Name for elder sister

Anna: Name for elder brother

Mangalsutra: A chain worn by Indian women signifying marital status

The Green Grass

Amma: Name for mother

Appa: Name for father

Subzi: Another name for vegetables in India

Ambujam Mami

Patti: A name for grandmother

Kanna: A loving name addressed to a young child

Agraharam: An exclusive settlement for Brahmins in southern India

Murruku: Traditional Indian savoury snack prepared with butter, rice and lentil flour

Tiffin: An evening snack

Porial: It is the Tamil word for fried or sometimes saute'd vegetable dish

Kootu: Lentil based Curries

Mysore pak: This is a sweet dish of Karnataka, India, usually served as dessert

Papadam: This is a thin, crisp Indian preparation sometimes described as a cracker

Mami: A name given to elderly ladies in southern India

Fit for a Queen

Dosa: or Dosai or is a fermented crepe or pancake made from rice batter and black lentils, very popular in southern India

Tambola: Bingo, which used to be known as Housey in the United Kingdom or *Tambola* in Asian countries

Goddess Kali: Kali is the Hindu Goddess who removes the ego and liberates the soul from the cycle of birth and death. Read about the *Goddess Kali* here.

No Stones Upturned

Mama: Maternal Uncle or Mother's Brother

Sai Baba bhakth: Devotees of Sai Baba

Finkler's question: A book written by Howard Jacobson

Reviews

Vinay Raj

17 April 13

An Honest and Unvarnished Look at Your Life

This book is about everyday people leading everyday lives. This book is about you. You are the character and the narrator, and you could be the author too. This book is not about superheroes, or wizards, or vampires, or detectives, or any of the million larger than life characters that seem to get churned out writers' imaginations these days like objects on a production line. The beauty of this book is in it's minimalism and simplicity, but do not underestimate the magnitude and depth of the underlying message in each page that you turn. Think of this book as a mirror. It will make you introspect. If you can look past the publisher's errors and lackluster presentation, the stories in this book carry words of weight and quality, and you will not regret having spent a few hours with the simple and charming beauty that is, 'No Stones Upturned'.

Sai Krishna

15 April 13

Short Simple Profound

I really love those days when simple, home cooked food is served deliciously without much of a fuss. 'No stones upturned' is exactly that. Every character, every story is maybe a person/incident from our own life. There is a great deal of familiarity in the the stories which helps us relate to the narrative. The stories are crisp, concise and leave us a lot of food for thought. I really loved the ambiguity of the themes/morals each story deals with - left open for the reader to infer which story is really about what. Having the privilege of being Ms. Subhashini's student for over four years, I must say she is one woman to watch out for. She is a treasure trove of perspectives, emotions, experience and confidence. Cant wait for more to come!

Akansha Goel

13 April 13

Blueprint of Real Life

No Stones Upturned.. The title only suggests that no matter how many trials and tribulations come in your way, they cannot change things until you allow them to make changes. I liked this book because of its light but deep feeling stories in which each story has a different moral but in short has a moral to be strong and believe in yourself. I personally feel that "Believe in yourself and the wheel of time will turn your way.." and this book somewhere reflects this belief of mine.. Loved to read it :)

It seriously is an insight into the life of a common man as this book is open to read for people of all ages..!! Good Work..

Expecting more books from the author :-)

Ruchismita

13 April 13

No Stones Upturned

No Stones Upturned is a different kind of book in this age of fiction and love stories. the stories are very simple yet they tell the truth about human life and emotions very vividly! i bet the reader will find atleast one story or a part of it that they can relate to in real life.

Joy Bakshi

12 April 13

Very Nice! Just Loved it !

A very nice and enjoyable book meant for readers of no particular age. A book which can fascinate an audience of any type and age and provide a nice flavor of Indian culture and an insight to a lot of indigenous stuff which even an Indian might be hearing about for the first time. It is a wonderful pack of stories providing moral teachings and values important for life. It is a guarantee, that every part of the book will not get you bored at any moment...A worth Read !

Chhavi Srivastav

12 April 13

Simplicity at its Best!

No Stones Upturned is an amazing book for those looking for a light reading experience. It provides the reader a break from life's monotony and offers a unique, delightful view of day to day activities.

The author wins brownie points by the use of easy, straightforward language and intelligent humor. While 'When times change' is written as a diary entry of a woman, and focuses on the social neglect faced by the common man/woman, 'God bless my darling' brings out the love of a mother, who with her positivity and efforts, pulls her daughter out of a terrible illness.

Where 'Ambujam Mami' forces the reader to introspect if the society has become more judge-mental, 'The night that changed my life' is a story of a young girl as she realizes the bitter truth of life .

A good combination of delicately chosen issues, the book sure is worth giving a shot.

Ayushi Sen

12 April 13

Loved It!

"Simple stories that leave a very deep message in our minds"

That is how i would describe this book. I generally like to read something light and interesting before going to sleep at night and this book had both the elements.

Each story was like a different spice - belonging to the same category but with a new and interesting flavour.

A must buy :)

Tanya Karanwal

12 April 13

Pretty Awsome

The stories are fresh & amazing.

Written in a simple yet crisp language, the book is alot fun to read.

I really liked the simplicity and effectiveness of "God bless my darling" One must try hands on this one. :)

This review was written for No Stones Upturned

Apoorv Singh

11 April 13

FIRST TO REVIEW

A Complete Insight into a Common Man's Life!

I don't Personally like thick bulky books! plus i am not a heavy reader who could sit bum stuck to couch for long hours to read about the imaginary world that was there in someone else's mind! I like reading Live n real Facts that exist in space and time! Being an Indian and a lazy student, i think this book is just made for ppl lik me! :P

Ten simple short stories you could read each day from various spheres of Typical indian life!

Awesome book a treat to young minds willing to get into a common man life! :D

Arohi Sharma

16 March 13

A Good Read!

I picked up this book by chance actually (was surfing through flipkart for short story collections) and I must say i am really happy with my purchase. All the ten stories are extremely insightful and they bring out the observative nature of the author. A fun read. I especially loved the story abt the teenager learning life's lessons in the course of a single night.

Not a criticism, just a suggestion:

A thorough proof reading of the book would have taken it to new heights! :)

Jay Zulu

10 October 12

FIRST TO REVIEW

Very Very Good Book

I Read this book as soon as i was able to get hold of it. It was all that I had expected from the Author Subhashini Ramakrishnan. It was a very fresh take on Indians who have got out of their comfort zone and have put their families ahead(shifting to new destinations, standing by physical ailments and many more). The writing is very simple yet crisp, with the language that will appeal to everyone.

For all the People who want a fresh read, this is a perfect choice.

RAPIDEX ENGLISH SPEAKING COURSE/EXCEL ENGLISH SPEAKING COURSE

ISBN : 9789381448908 (Telugu) | ISBN : 9789381448915 (Bangla) | ISBN : 9789381448922 (Oriya) | ISBN : 9789381448939 (Assamese) | ISBN : 9789381448946 (Nepalese)

Published in sixteen languages
Hindi, Malayalam, Tamil, Telugu, Kannada, Marathi, Gujarati, Bangla, Oriya, Urdu, Assamese, Punjabi, Nepalese, Persian, Arabic and Sinhalese

REGIONAL LANGUAGE/SPOKEN ENGLISH/LEARNING COURSES

ISBN : 9789357940054 (Bangla) | ISBN : 9789357940016 (Bangla) | ISBN :9789357940023 (Bangla) | ISBN : 9789357940085 (Bangla) | ISBN : 9789357940825 (Bangla) | ISBN : 9789357940092 (Bangla) | ISBN : 9789357940009 (Bangla) | ISBN : 9789357940030 (Bangla) | ISBN : 9789357941303 *(2 Colour Book)*

ISBN : 9789357940061 (Bangla) | ISBN : 9789357940047 (Bangla) | ISBN : 9788122310924 (Bangla) | ISBN : 9789357940078 (Bangla) | ISBN 9789350570357 (Kannada) | ISBN : 9789350571200 (Kannada) | ISBN : 9789350570340 (Kannada) | ISBN : 9789350570944 (Kannada) | *(Coming Soon)* Marathi

ISBN : 9789350570951 (Kannada) | ISBN : 9789350571309 (Kannada) | ISBN : 9789350571828 (Gujarati) | ISBN : 9789350571781 (Gujarati) | ISBN : 9789350571811 (Marathi) | ISBN : 9789350571804 (Marathi) | ISBN : 9789381384138 (Tamil) | ISBN : 9789381384121 (Tamil) | *(Coming Soon)* Punjabi

ISBN : 9789357940153 (Eng.-Bangla) | ISBN : 9789357940399 (Eng.-Kannada) | ISBN : 9789357940375 (Eng.-Odia) | ISBN : 9789357940382 (Eng.-Telugu) | ISBN : 9789357941358 (Eng.-Malayalam) | ISBN : 9789357941327 (Eng.-Tamil) | ISBN : 9789357940856 (Eng.-Marathi) | ISBN : 9789357940849 (Eng.-Gujarati) | *(Coming Soon)* Kannada

ISBN : 9789357941334 (Eng.-Assamese) | ISBN : 9789357941341 (Eng.-Urdu) | ISBN : 9789350570760 (Telugu) | ISBN : 9789350570098 (Telugu) | ISBN : 9789350571699 (Bangla) | ISBN : 9789350571125 (Bangla) | ISBN : 9789357940146 (Kannada) | ISBN : 9789357940139 (Kannada) | *(Coming Soon)* Gujarati

ISBN : 9789350571620 (Odia) | ISBN : 9789350571118 (Odia) | ISBN : 9789350570982 (Marathi) | ISBN : 9789350571835 (Marathi) | ISBN : 9789357940795 Bangla | ISBN : 9789357940801 Odia | ISBN : 9789357940818 Telugu

All Books Available on Flipkart, Amazon, Infibeam, Snapdeal, Shopcluse • marketing@vspublishers.com

V&S OLYMPIAD SERIES FOR CLASSES 1-10

MATHS OLYMPIAD (CLASS 1-10)

ISBN : 9789357940504 ISBN : 9789357940511 ISBN : 9789357940528 ISBN : 9789357940535 ISBN : 9789357940542

ISBN : 9789357940559 ISBN : 9789357940566 ISBN : 9789357940573 ISBN : 9789357940580 ISBN : 9789357940597

SCIENCE OLYMPIAD (CLASS 1-10)

ISBN : 9789357940405 ISBN : 9789357940412 ISBN : 9789357940429 ISBN : 9789357940436 ISBN : 9789357940443

ISBN : 9789357940450 ISBN : 9789357940467 ISBN : 9789357940474 ISBN : 9789357940481 ISBN : 9789357940498

CYBER OLYMPIAD (CLASS 1-10)

ISBN : 9789357942102 ISBN : 9789357940603 ISBN : 9789357940610 ISBN : 9789357940627 ISBN : 9789357940634

ISBN : 9789357940641 ISBN : 9789357940658 ISBN : 9789357940665 ISBN : 9789357940672 ISBN : 9789357940689

ENGLISH OLYMPIAD (CLASS 1-10)

ISBN : 9789357940696 ISBN : 9789357940702 ISBN : 9789357940719 ISBN : 9789357940726 ISBN : 9789357940733

ISBN : 9789357940740 ISBN : 9789357940757 ISBN : 9789357940764 ISBN : 9789357940771 ISBN : 9789357940788

OLYMPIAD ONLINE TEST PACKAGE (CLASS 1-10)

ISBN : 9789357941754 ISBN : 9789357941761 ISBN : 9789357941778 ISBN : 978935794

ISBN : 9789357941792 ISBN : 9789357941808 ISBN : 9789357941815 ISBN : 978935794

ISBN : 9789357941839 ISBN : 9789357941846

OLYMPIAD ONLINE TEST PACKAG
CLASS 1-10
with CD with Activation Voucher
web Portal: www.vsexamprep.cor

OLYMPIAD COMBO PACK (4 BOOK SET)

ISBN : 9789357942003 ISBN : 9789357942010 ISBN : 9789357942027

ISBN : 9789357942034 ISBN : 9789357942041 ISBN : 9789357942058

ISBN : 9789357942065 ISBN : 9789357942072 ISBN : 9789357942089

ISBN : 9789357942096

CLASS 1-10 ENGLISH, MATHS,
CYBER, SCIENCE OLYMPIAD
4 BOOKS SAVER COMBO PACK